CAN GEORGINA'S FOOTMAN MASQUERADE AS A PRINCE?

"Why, I wager that I could convince them that even a footman was a prince of the blood..."

"What an intriquing idea," said Sir Swithin Baxter with his usual grin. "Even a footman you say?"

"Yes!" declared Georgina, "I daresay I could."

Penelope also seemed intrigued by the idea. "I don't know. Some footmen, perhaps, but you certainly couldn't turn that ruffian we met yesterday into a proper gentleman."

HOW LONG CAN LORD HUGH MASQUERADE AS A FOOTMAN?

ROGUE'S MASQUERADE

MARGARET SUMMERVILLE

AVON
PUBLISHERS OF BARD, CAMELOT, DISCUS AND FLARE BOOKS

ROGUE'S MASQUERADE is an original publication of Avon Books. This work has never before appeared in book form.

AVON BOOKS
A division of
The Hearst Corporation
959 Eighth Avenue
New York, New York 10019

Copyright © 1981 by Margaret Summerville
Published by arrangement with the author
Library of Congress Catalog Card Number: 80-69948
ISBN: 0-380-78469-6

All rights reserved, which includes the right to reproduce this book or portions thereof in any form whatsoever except as provided by the U.S. Copyright Law. For information address Tandem Press Publishers, Tannersville, Pennsylvania 18372

First Avon Printing, September, 1981

AVON TRADEMARK REG. U.S. PAT. OFF. AND IN OTHER COUNTRIES, MARCA REGISTRADA, HECHO EN U.S.A.

Printed in the U.S.A.

10 9 8 7 6 5 4 3 2 1

To Ashley and Isabelle Wilson

ROGUE'S MASQUERADE

1

JIMMY SMALLBONE LOOKED AT HIS WATCH and frowned. It was getting late, and there was still no sign of his master's cousin. "Blasted public coaches!" he muttered as he carefully deposited the watch back into his pocket. Smallbone thought it abominable that a lord of the realm should have to travel in such a common way. And his father a duke and rich as Croesus, too, he reflected, shaking his head. Suddenly there was a shout from the crowd, and Smallbone looked up.

"Here she comes!" cried a jolly, inebriated fellow whose pleasure it was to pass his idle hours hailing the arrival of coaches. Smallbone inched his way through the crowd so he could get a better view as the coach appeared and clattered to a halt. He waited impatiently as the coachman jumped down and opened the door.

The first passenger to alight was a plump, middle-aged woman, who, to Smallbone's mind, made a most undignified shriek as she spied a waiting relative in the crowd. She was followed by two sober-faced gentlemen and an amiable-looking man in clerical garb. The last person to get off the coach was a young, dark gentleman. Smallbone sighed in relief and hurried up to meet him.

"M'lord," he said, and the young gentleman looked at him and smiled.

"Smallbone," said the gentleman in a cultivated voice with a hint of a north country accent. "I'm glad to see you. How have you been?"

"Fine, m'lord," said Smallbone, who had some difficulty disguising his dismay at the young man's appearance.

At that moment Hugh Ballanville, ninth Marquis of Renwick, did not at all look like the heir to a dukedom. His rough, shabby clothes were better suited to a coachman, and he was covered with dust. His face was unshaven, and his curly black hair fell about his forehead in wild disarray. However, despite the marquis's sorry attire and unkempt appearance, Smallbone noted that he was quite handsome. Renwick was taller than average height, with broad shoulders and a muscular, athletic build. His face was distinguished by strong, clear-cut features and blue eyes that often held a look of mischievous amusement.

Deciding that the marquis's appearance would soon be remedied by his stay in town, Smallbone returned to the task at hand. "We best get your luggage, m'lord."

"Of course," said Renwick, and the two men approached the pile of boxes that was materializing from the top of the coach. The sight of the marquis's luggage further dismayed Smallbone, for sorrier bags he had never seen. He dutifully transferred them to his master's carriage and turned to his lordship.

"We'd best be off, then, m'lord."

"Gladly, Smallbone," said the marquis, looking over at the carriage and then back at the servant. "I should like to drive. It was a damnable ride in that cramped coach, and I should be grateful for the fresh air and a hand at the ribbons."

Smallbone smiled. "Of course, m'lord." He had heard much of his lordship's skill as a driver and was not at all concerned with turning the reins over to him, even though his lordship was not used to the congested streets of London. Indeed, although he was six and twenty, it was Lord Renwick's first trip to town, a fact that Smallbone found quite shocking. For a young gentleman like Renwick to be stranded up in a Godforsaken northern province, deprived of the civilizing influences of London, was simply dreadful.

Renwick took the reins and maneuvered the vehicle out into the busy street. For a time they rode in silence, Renwick intent on the London scene. He finally turned to Smallbone.

"And so this is the great city, is it, Smallbone?"

"Aye, m'lord."

"Damned lot of people around. Never saw so many since the Lennonshire fair."

"Indeed, m'lord," replied Smallbone, trying to hide his shock at hearing the great city of London compared to a country fair.

"But how is my cousin?"

"Very well, m'lord. Mr. Ballanville is very happy you were able to come to London for his wedding."

"Good old Vic. I'll be glad to see him again, although at the moment I don't know whether I'll be gladder to see him or a bath."

Smallbone smiled. "It was quite a long journey here, m'lord."

"Aye, it was a long journey, indeed." As he said these words, a curricle went charging past them from the other direction, and he whistled. "They drive a bit wild hereabouts, don't they, Smallbone?" Just as his lordship was making this observation, a high-perch phaeton came around a corner at breakneck speed. To Renwick's surprise, the driver of the vehicle was a lady. Dressed in a bright pink dress, she was merrily urging her horses to go faster and faster. He caught a glimpse of another lady beside her, who, sharing her companion's high spirits, was laughing gleefully. The vehicle tilted dangerously as it made the corner, and the galloping horses headed straight for Renwick's carriage.

"God damn!" cried the marquis. Turning his horses sharply and pulling them up short, he narrowly avoided a collision. The phaeton had come within inches of his horses, but it continued blithely down the street, careening around another vehicle and then finally hitting a small fruit cart, sending apples and peaches flying into the air.

Renwick cursed again and, handing the reins to Smallbone, jumped down from the carriage. He angrily made his way to where the phaeton had come to a halt amid the strewn fruit. Smallbone watched him in alarm, having heard that the marquis had inherited the Ballanville temper and could be hotheaded.

"What the devil do you think you're doing? Someone could've been killed by your damned foolishness," Lord Renwick shouted, looking up at the phaeton's passengers. He was somewhat taken aback by the appearance of these two would-be Amazons who had exhibited such reckless and dangerous conduct.

The driver of the vehicle, who was attired in a fashionable pink dress and wore a hat with large plum-colored feathers, appeared quite unconcerned about the matter. She regarded Renwick with an expression of haughty disapproval that infuriated the marquis even more. Yet, even in his fury, Renwick could not help but notice that she was most attractive. Her oval face, with its pale complexion and classical features dominated by remarkable brown eyes, proclaimed her to be one of the beauties of society.

"Whom do you think you are addressing?" she said, fixing her enormous eyes upon him. "How dare you speak so to ladies!"

"Indeed," contributed her companion, and Renwick's glance shifted. In contrast to her dark companion, this delicate beauty had blond hair and blue eyes.

Renwick, in his anger, was immune to the ladies' obvious feminine charms. "Ladies, eh? By my way of thinking, ladies don't rush about the streets like a pair o' damned Huns." In his anger Renwick's speech had taken on a more noticeable north country accent.

The dark-eyed lady frowned. "My good man," she said, "I suggest you calm yourself and reflect upon your lack of manners."

"Lack o' manners? Is it good manners to drive like a drunken coachman, nearly killing everyone in the street? Damm lucky you didn't break your fool neck."

By this time there was a considerable crowd gathering around the phaeton, and the lady looked at the curious faces and then back at Renwick. She kept her voice low, but there was fury in her dark eyes.

"You are insolent! And I would thank you not to use such language."

"And I would thank you, miss, to watch what you are doing," shouted Renwick.

"Really, my good fellow," said the blond lady in a languid voice. "I don't see why you are so excited. Oh dear. Was it *your* fruit wagon, then?"

"No, it wasn't! I was driving the carriage you damn near ran into back there." Renwick motioned toward the carriage, and the lady glanced back in that direction.

She spied the carriage and also observed Smallbone, then turned to her companion in surprise. "Why, Georgie, I believe it's Victor's man."

That worthy servant had received quite a shock on recognizing the occupants of the phaeton and had been staring speechlessly at them. However, he now came to his senses and, leaving the reins with an obliging youth, hastened over.

As he approached them, he gave a deferential nod. "Good day, miss," he said to the blond lady, and then, turning to her companion, "M'lady."

"Tell me, Smallbone," said the blond lady, "when did Mr. Ballanville employ such an insolent ruffian?" She looked over at Renwick and added meaningfully, "He won't be employed much longer, I daresay."

"But you don't understand, miss," began Smallbone, looking quite embarrassed, "this here is—"

Renwick cut him off abruptly. "The ladies aren't interested in who I am." Jimmy Smallbone looked dumbfounded, at his lordship.

By this time an even larger crowd had gathered and was finding the scene quite entertaining—all save for a poor stooped-shouldered old woman, who began sobbing about the damage to her fruit cart.

"Oh, good heavens," cried the dark lady, "I will pay you for your cart." She reached in her reticule and threw down a few coins to the woman, who quickly stopped sobbing and grinned as she eagerly counted the coins in her hand.

"So you pay the poor woman a few coins and think all is forgiven," said Renwick sarcastically.

"Stand aside, if you will. I do not wish to continue this conversation. Mr. Ballanville will hear of your behavior, I warn you."

"Now wait just a moment," cried Renwick.

The dark-eyed lady raised her whip menacingly at him. "Stand aside or I will teach you some manners." Renwick scowled, but stood aside, and she flicked the reins and gave him one last withering look as the phaeton resumed its journey. The marquis watched them drive off and then turned to Smallbone.

"Good God, Smallbone, what a pair of harpies! Egad,

I've never seen such dreadful females. If they are examples of London ladies, I think I had best return north."

"My lord," said Smallbone weakly. "Those ladies . . ."

Renwick looked at Smallbone and noted that he looked quite ill. "What is wrong, Smallbone?"

The servant cleared his throat. "The dark-haired lady is Lady Georgina Suttondale, sister to the Earl of Rumbridge."

"I care nothing for who she is."

"But m'lord, the other lady was her cousin, Miss Penelope Amesbury." Smallbone hesitated. "Miss Amesbury is Mr. Ballanville's betrothed."

Hugh Ballanville, Marquis of Renwick, looked at Smallbone in astonishment. "You mean . . . she is the Miss Amesbury who is to marry my cousin?"

"Yes, m'lord."

"Good God!" cried his lordship.

"Precisely, m'lord," sighed Smallbone.

As she entered her cousin's house, Lady Georgina Suttondale took off her plumed hat, revealing shiny black curls. Lady Georgina was very proud of her hair, which was perfectly suited to the current fashion and greatly admired. "Do you believe the impudence of the man, cousin?" said Lady Georgina, shaking her head. "Shouting at us like that! And in front of all those people. I have never been so insulted."

Her cousin looked over at her and smiled. "Do calm down, Georgie. That is all you have talked about since we left that unfortunate street. If only that wretched old woman had had the good sense to keep her fruit cart out of our way."

"Oh, the poor woman," said Lady Georgina. "I do feel bad about that."

"Nonsense, you paid her far more than the cart was worth."

"That fellow did not think I had done so."

"Oh, we are back to him again, are we? I agree that he was a dreadful ruffian, and I can't imagine my Victor hiring him. But I must admit, he was terribly good looking."

"Good looking?"

"Oh, Georgie, don't act as though you didn't notice. A

dark romantic rogue he was. A bit rough, of course, and unkempt; but those blue eyes, cousin! Did you not think them the bluest eyes you had ever seen?"

"Penelope! What nonsense," said Lady Georgina, sitting down in an elegant sofa in the drawing room. "I did not note the color of the fellow's eyes."

Penelope cast her cousin a sly look. "Did you find him so unattractive, coz?"

"Yes," Georgina declared stoutly. Penelope laughed, and Georgina smiled.

"Oh, all right, I confess he was not unattractive. But the insolence of the man! I daresay I am not accustomed to servants treating me so."

"Yes, well, I shall have to talk to my dear old Vic about him," said Penelope. "If he is to remain in Victor's employ, which is doubtful at best, he must learn to know his place. But let us not talk any more of him. We have more important matters to discuss, such as my new dress for the Bedfords' ball. Georgie, I am not at all happy with it. Oh, I loved it at first, but now I am not so certain it is quite the thing. You must help me. Come let us go and see it."

"Very well, cousin," said Lady Georgina, rising from the sofa and following Penelope from the drawing room. But as she left the room, a vision of the rough stranger came to her mind. He *did* have blue eyes, reflected Lady Georgina; but she quickly admonished herself to put all thoughts of the insufferable man from her mind and ascended the stairs to her cousin's rooms.

The Marquis of Renwick was very glad to arrive at the fashionable townhouse that was the London home of his cousin, the Honorable Victor Ballanville. His first hours in London had not endeared him to that city, and he was eager to see his cousin's much-beloved face. Having four sisters but no brothers, Lord Renwick regarded his cousin Victor as the brother he had never had. They were of the same age and had always got on famously, somehow avoiding the seemingly inevitable conflicts that marred many brotherly relationships.

From the time he was seven years old, Victor Ballanville had journeyed with his parents to Ballanville Castle, near the Scottish border, a brooding edifice of stone that was the ancestral home of the Ballanvilles since the twelfth century. Young Renwick had always looked forward to his cousin's annual visits, and although he had always longed to visit Victor, it was not until now that he had been able to do so.

Renwick's father, the Duke of Welham, had adamantly opposed his son's wishes to go to London. A stern and somewhat eccentric personage, the duke stoutly maintained that his son might not journey to the great southern city until he had attained the age of six and twenty. How he had decided upon this age was a mystery to Renwick, who had since his eighteenth birthday argued and pleaded with his father to allow him to see London. Yet the duke had prevailed, and Renwick's taste of big-city life had been limited to trips to Edinburgh, a city he loved but knew was quite barbarous compared to London.

"There's the house, m'lord," said Smallbone, gesturing toward a row of elegant brick buildings. "That is Mr. Ballanville's house. The second one there." Renwick pulled the horses up to the curb and handed the reins to Smallbone.

"Do go ahead, m'lord," said the servant. "Mr. Ballanville is eager to see you."

Renwick nodded. He hopped down from the driver's seat and knocked upon the door, using the brass door knocker. The door opened and Renwick grinned to see his cousin Victor.

"Hugh, old fellow!" cried Victor Ballanville, impulsively embracing his cousin at the doorstep. "Dashed good to see you!" He released the marquis and ushered him inside. "It's been so long, cousin. Too damned long, I'd say. Come in, come in."

Victor led his cousin to the drawing room and hurried to pour him a glass of sherry. His lordship accepted it gratefully and looked appreciatively around the room. What a contrast it presented from the dreary rooms at Ballanville Castle. It was light and airy and filled with elegant furniture and potted palms, and Renwick could not help but think his cousin a very lucky man.

"You have grown taller, Hugh," said Victor. "If only I might have grown a few inches. I fear I am too short to be taken seriously in society. But, my dear fellow, I fear your tailor does not do you credit."

Renwick laughed. "It is you who is the man of society, not I, Vic. I'll wager you're the best-dressed man in London."

"Nonsense," said Victor Ballanville, glowing with pleasure at his cousin's praise. But, indeed, he devoted most of his waking hours to the pursuit of sartorial elegance. The rest of his time he devoted to avoiding the creditors who were forever dunning him for the extravagant sums he paid to remain a man of fashion.

Renwick had always admired his cousin's appearance. Although Victor claimed he was short, he was of average height, and his trim figure and boyish good looks were acclaimed among the ladies. Renwick noted Victor's precisely fitted coat, his elegant white pantaloons and gleaming boots. Although his cousin's elaborately tied neck cloth seemed a bit overdone to his lordship's provincial eye, he regarded Victor Ballanville's attire with undisguised envy.

"I feel like a ragged rooster beside a peacock," said his lordship. "You must think me quite a sight."

Victor made a comical face. "You do look a sight, old boy. A damned welcome sight, I might add! God, it's good to see you, Hugh."

"And it's good to see you, cousin. Dashed if it wasn't even worth that damnable coach ride to see you again!"

Victor Ballanville shook his head and took a sip of sherry. "Really, cousin, to come by public coach! Not quite the thing, you know."

"Well, it might not be quite the thing, Vic, but it was the only way I could get here. I would never have made it in any of my father's antique carriages."

Victor laughed. "Oh God, the duke and his carriages. I daresay all of them were built shortly after the invention of the wheel! And my uncle still refuses to buy a new one?"

Renwick slumped down wearily on the sofa and grinned. "You know the duke. He says buying a new carriage would be extravagant when the old ones are still in such good condition."

"Good condition? The last time I was at Ballanville Castle I rode in one of those aged vehicles, and I was sore for days. I mean it really is abominable, Hugh. Doesn't the duke ever spend any of his blunt? Egad, he's got enough of it!"

The Marquis of Renwick smiled. "Oh, father just doesn't believe in being a spendthrift."

Victor shook his head, but decided not to comment further. His uncle was an eccentric, all right, living like some accursed miser despite his vast wealth. Victor was appalled by anyone having all that money and not enjoying it. However, his cousin Hugh, though at times exasperated by his father's frugality, was usually merely amused by it.

Victor decided to change the subject and asked about his cousin's family. After hearing the latest news of the north country Ballanvilles, Victor shook his head. "I still can't believe you're actually here in London. After so many years the duke has finally allowed you to come! But you have reached the magic age of six and twenty, as I have myself. Oh, we are growing old!" Victor sat down beside the marquis. "I must admit, Hugh, I half suspected his grace would change his mind and keep you hidden away in the northlands. And I should never have forgiven him if he had not allowed you to come to my wedding.

Renwick smiled. "Oh, my father was quite willing to allow me to come. In fact he urged me to come."

"The devil!"

"He did indeed. It was a great surprise to me, but he informed me two weeks ago that I had come of an age when I might think of marriage. He said I might do well to follow your example."

"My example? Oh that is a rare one, Hugh. If I recall, my uncle thinks of me as a fop and a coxcomb. He said as much to me; but do not worry, Hugh, I do not care at all for my noble uncle's opinion."

"Very sensible."

"But he wants you to marry, then?"

Renwick nodded. "You may recall that my father visited London only once in thirty-one years. That was when he met my mother and spirited her off to Ballanville Castle."

"And he expects you to do the same? By God, this is famous. What lucky damsel shall it be?"

"Don't be ridiculous."

Victor laughed. "Well, there are many eligible ladies,

and we shall find you one easily enough. Wait until I show you about town. What a lark we'll have."

Renwick smiled, but reflected that after his long journey all he wanted was a hot bath and a soft bed. As if he read his cousin's mind, Victor suddenly became solicitous.

"But dammit, Hugh, here I am going on and on and you look weary to death. I'll have Smallbone get you a bath and something to eat. We'll wait till tomorrow to go larking about. Of course, you'll have to meet Penelope, my fiancée."

"Oh yes," said Renwick, with a slight smile.

"You know, old boy, I didn't even tell her you were coming. Thought I'd surprise her. I tell you, Hugh, you'll adore Penelope. Just don't adore her too much, mind you. She is absolutely wonderful, and I know it is dreadfully sentimental of me, but I am mad about her. My Penelope is a remarkable lady—but you will find that out when you meet her."

The marquis folded his arms in front of him. "I fear I did meet her, cousin."

"What? You have only just arrived!"

Renwick smiled. "You might say we met by accident, or near-accident. She was riding with a Lady Georgina, who is an absolute terror at the reins! She nearly drove into your carriage on the way over here."

"The devil!"

"Yes, and then she did hit an old woman's cart. But no one was injured, thank God!"

Victor sat down. "And Georgina was driving? By God, she is usually the more sensible of the two. I shan't let Penelope near that phaeton when we're married." Lord Renwick looked skeptical, and his cousin laughed. "I see you think Penelope ain't the sort to take orders, and you're right! I won't get to act lord and master with her. But that's one of the reasons I love her. I like a lady with spirit. What did you think of my Penelope?"

Renwick smiled. "She's quite a beauty, cousin. That much was obvious."

"Oh, she's a beauty, all right. And she's also an adorable lunatic. I do hope you like her, cousin."

"Since you are so dashed fond of her, Vic, I know I shall be devoted to the lady. But I fear I did not make a very good impression on her. To put it bluntly, I made a mess of it!"

"Did you?" asked Victor, with a smile.

"I lost my temper, you see—"

"Oh no, the terrible Ballanville temper," said Victor in melodramatic tones.

His cousin grinned. "Although it was not entirely my fault. I fear your lady's friend was the most insufferable female I have ever met."

"Georgina? She is adorable."

"As adorable as a maddened bull."

"My dear Hugh, hardly a flattering comparison. Lady Georgina is a bit high spirited, as is my Penelope. She is Penelope's cousin."

"Yes, so poor Smallbone informed me later. She called me an insolent fellow. By God, Vic, she and your Penelope thought me a ruffian and came to the conclusion that I was a new servant you had hired."

Victor looked amazed. "You, a new servant?" And he suddenly burst out laughing.

"Oh, you may think it's funny, cousin," said the Marquis, with a serious expression, "but I damn well think she intends to have me dismissed."

Victor Ballanville laughed even louder at this, and his cousin joined in. "My poor Hugh," said Victor, "I find it hard to believe they did not recognize you as a gentleman, although I must admit your attire scarcely befits your station. But don't worry, Hugh, we shall set the matter at rights tomorrow. Oh, I shall quiz Penelope unmercifully. She shall regret not recognizing my cousin for the noble lord he is. Georgina will think it very amusing."

"Perhaps, but I don't thank that lady and I shall ever make amends. I believe she disliked me as heartily as I disliked her."

"Dislike Georgina? My dear old cousin, I had thought that impossible. Georgina Suttondale is the toast of society. There is hardly a gentleman in town who is not in love with her, and the prince is so terribly fond of her. Perhaps she is a bit wild, but that is rather the fashion."

"Is it? But she seemed a spoiled brat."

"Really, cousin," protested Victor. "Do not form your opinions too hastily. Remember what the ladies thought about you."

Renwick grinned. "You're right, Vic. Go on."

"Well," said Victor, "Georgina's father, the old earl, was devoted to her. He took her everywhere with him. Taught her to ride and hunt and drive."

"He made a mess of that, it seems," remarked Renwick.

"Oh, she's a very skilled driver. I've seen her handle a four-in-hand easy as you please. And she's damned good at all manner of cards."

"Hardly fit accomplishments for a lady."

"Oh, don't be so dashed straitlaced, Hugh. Yes, I can remember her as a girl. Tearing about town with her papa. A little hoyden, she was."

"And apparently still is," said the Marquis, frowning.

"Oh, she's gotten a bit steadier, but then the last couple of years haven't been easy for her. Old Rumbridge died two years ago and she went to live with her brother. Young Rumbridge is a difficult, priggish fellow, and his wife is most disagreeable, too. And they have a pair of sons, dreadful brats who fortunately for Georgina are in school now. But, Egad, Hugh, here I go telling you Georgina's life history and you're not at all interested."

Lord Renwick smiled and reflected with some surprise that he had been quite interested in hearing about Lady Georgina Suttondale. However, he decided that he would be quite content if he never met such an aggravating female again.

2

IT WAS LATE AFTERNOON WHEN LADY GEORgina Suttondale returned to the home of her brother, Robert, fifth Earl of Rumbridge. As usual, Georgina returned reluctantly. It was well known among society that Lady Georgina and her brother did not get on very well. They were separated not only by a fifteen-year difference in ages but also by a difference in temperament so drastic that most of those acquainted with the family found it hard to believe they could be brother and sister.

The earl was a serious man who lived a sober, quiet life and who disliked most people and took great pains to avoid them. He abhorred society and would have been content to spend the season in the country if his wife, Amelia, had not insisted they come to town. Lord Rumbridge was known as one of the greatest bores and most disagreeable of gentlemen, and most hostesses were relieved when he declined their invitation.

Amelia was only slightly better regarded in society. Because she was the sister of one of the most dreaded patronesses of Almack's, Lady Rumbridge's position was secure, despite her reputation as a spiteful, unpleasant woman. She was humorless and often malicious and had formed an early aversion toward her husband's young sister. Lady Rumbridge thought Georgina frivolous, unladylike, and very likely to bring disgrace upon the family.

Georgina did have some affection for her brother, but none at all for Lady Rumbridge. And, therefore, she entered her brother's house with her usual misgivings. Even so, she tried to be cheerful, greeting her brother's butler with a smile.

"Good afternoon, Tabb."

The butler smiled back at her and nodded. "Good day, m'lady." Tabb was quite fond of the Lady Georgina, having been in service to the Suttondale family all his life and having known her since she was an infant. He hated to see her sunny smile disappear, but he had no choice in the matter. "His lordship wishes to see your ladyship in the library."

As the butler had foreseen, the smile immediately faded. Tabb nodded sympathetically, and Lady Georgina sighed. Whenever her brother wanted to see her in the library, it meant trouble. The Earl of Rumbridge reserved the library for serious business matters, and one of these included the lecturing of his young and, to his mind, wayward sister. When Georgina opened the door to the library, her fears were confirmed, for her brother looked up from his desk and regarded her disapprovingly.

The Earl of Rumbridge was seven and thirty, but he appeared older than his years. He shared the dark hair and eyes of his young sister, but his features were rather sharp and his expression constantly grim.

"Georgina," he pronounced in a stern voice.

"Really, Robert, you do look forbidding. What have I done now?"

He frowned. "Sit down, Georgina."

"As you command, brother," she replied, sitting down in one of the uncomfortable chairs next to his desk. "All right, Robert, you may begin the lecture."

The Earl of Rumbridge observed her for a few moments and then shook his head. "Come now, Georgina, you are two and twenty, are you not? Too old for me to lecture as if you were a schoolgirl."

"How glad I am to hear that, Robert," said Georgina with a smile.

The earl stood up and walked over to the window. As he looked out the window he spoke with his back to her.

"I am told you went driving with Penelope this afternoon."

"Yes."

He turned back to her and frowned. "Don't you think it unseemly for two ladies to drive a phaeton about the streets of London?"

"Unseemly?"

"Yes, unseemly and unladylike."

"Oh really, Robert, don't be such an old stick."

"Call me what you will, Georgina, but you know I'm only concerned about your reputation. And driving about town in a phaeton with Penelope Amesbury can only do damage to it! That female delights in shocking people."

"Well, shocking people can be rather fun," said Georgina, and she burst out laughing at her brother's horrified expression.

"I see that you find this all very amusing, my girl, but you might at least show a little regard for your own marital prospects, if not for the good name of your family. Men might be amused by outrageous females who drive wildly about town in phaetons, but they aren't about to marry them!"

Georgina smiled. "Then what about Cousin Penelope and Victor?"

Rumbridge shook his head. "It is well known that Victor Ballanville has no money. And my wild cousin Penelope is frightfully rich, is she not? I think that should explain it."

Georgina's eyes flashed. "How dare you say such a thing, Rumbridge! Victor is not a fortune hunter! He loves Penelope."

Rumbridge smiled patronizingly at her. "Georgina, I know how fond you are of your cousin, but you really must begin to show some sense. Penelope Amesbury is not a fit companion for you. She has the most shocking manner for a female I have ever seen. And the company she keeps!" Rumbridge shook his head. "Artists, actors, and all manner of lowborn persons find their way to the Amesbury house. And she has no supervision! That uncle of hers who is her guardian, why the man cares nothing about what the girl does! She is not yet twenty, and that fool Roger Amesbury thinks nothing of allowing her to establish her own household with only that poor Mrs. Grove to lend countenance to the situation. It is disgraceful." The earl hesitated. "And since I am speaking of this, I have heard that you are showing too much attention toward a certain person."

Georgina was still angry, but this statement and her brother's look of acute embarrassment intrigued her.

"What 'person' would that be, Rumbridge?"

"That fellow Richard Averton. I tell you, my girl, Averton isn't the sort for you." The earl hesitated, but Georgina remained silent. Richard Averton was nothing more than a friend to her, but she had no intention of reassuring her brother of that. The earl continued. "I tell you, that Averton fellow puts on airs as if he were the equal to the prince himself. Yes, he acts the part of a gentleman, but he can't fool me."

"He can't?"

"Most assuredly not. The fellow is of dubious birth. I am told his father was a haberdasher—or worse."

"Oh dear!" exclaimed Georgina with a look of mock horror. "Worse than a haberdasher!"

"You may joke, my girl, but Averton is not for you. I know breeding when I see it, and no amount of polish can disguise the lowborn." He paused and then proclaimed solemnly. "Breeding always tells."

"Always?"

"Yes. So I hope you take heed of my advice. I am elder than you, after all, and wiser in the ways of the world. You are two and twenty and must soon take a husband. I have lately been giving careful consideration to the matter."

"You have?" said Georgina, controlling an urge to laugh.

"Of course. You have rejected many suitable gentlemen in the past, but I warn you, Georgina, the time has come for you to do your duty and marry as befits your station. I have someone in mind, a gentleman of birth and fortune who is in every way perfect for you."

"Really? Pray tell, who is this paragon?"

"Viscount Milford."

Georgina met this announcement with a look of astonishment, and then, quite abruptly, she burst into laughter. "Lord Milford? Really, Robert, you believe Milford to be the perfect husband?"

Her brother was extremely displeased by her reaction. "I don't see what is so amusing, Georgina. Lord Milford is a peer and his family, though not as illustrious as our own, is most acceptable. His fortune, though not great, is quite adequate, too, and I would say he has a sterling character."

"A sterling character?" Georgina repeated incredulously,

and then laughed again. "Why, Robert, the man is a pompous ass."

"Georgina," said the earl angrily. "I will not have any more of your impertinence. You forget that you are in my house and under my authority."

"How can I forget it when I am constantly reminded of it?" returned Georgina. "I am sorry I am such a burden to you!"

"Nonsense, Georgina, I just want what's best for you."

"And you think it best for me to saddle myself with a fool like Milford?"

"I suppose you'd prefer a fortune hunter like Averton."

"I should even prefer a haberdasher!" she cried, and stormed out of the room. The Earl of Rumbridge watched her go and frowned. It would be a difficult task getting his sister suitably married. She was stubborn and willful and cared nothing for her duty or his authority. Rumbridge frowned again.

No, my dear sister, he thought. This time you shall obey me. Milford is willing to have you, and have you he will. Rumbridge nodded resolutely and returned to his desk.

Georgina sat down upon her bed and shook her head. Why was her brother so difficult? she asked herself. Why was he so cold hearted, caring nothing for her feelings? Indeed, all he cared about was his illustrious rank and precious duty. She sighed and reflected that it was sometimes burdensome to be a great lady. How much easier life might be had she been born into a nice middle-class home, the daughter of a merchant or craftsman. Then she would not have to worry about making a grand marriage to someone like Lord Milford. Indeed, she might marry for love, as Penelope insisted the lower orders did with regularity.

Georgina laughed at herself. She knew very well that it was nonsense. She loved her position as an earl's daughter and lady of fashion. She loved to have new gowns and attend parties and talk to amusing people. In fact, before her father had died, she had been so very happy. Georgina nodded. Yes, in spite of her brother, she was far better off than women who did not share her lofty social position and who were doomed to marry such fellows as that impudent servant of Victor Ballanville's she had met that day. Georgina frowned suddenly. "Why do I think of him?" she said aloud. "He is but an impudent servant!" Vowing that she would not waste one more thought on the man, Georgina got up and rang for her maid. Her summons was quickly answered by a smiling young woman who expressed no surprise at her mistress's announcement that she was not going down to dinner. Sally Jenkins knew her mistress well and, like the other servants in the household, had quickly learned that their master and his sister had been quarreling again. Sally thought it terrible how Lord Rumbridge treated his sister, who in Sally's eyes could do no wrong.

"Would you be wanting a tray then, m'lady?"

Georgina smiled conspiratorially at her maid. "Later, Sally. Since you are to inform his lordship I have no appetite, the tray had best wait until they are at dinner."

"Yes, my lady."

Georgina, aided by her maid, changed her clothes and settled down for a night of reading.

The next morning brought with it the promise of a beautiful spring day, and as Lady Georgina looked out her window, her spirits were somewhat restored. Her argument with her brother had at first angered and then depressed her. Georgina hated being obligated to her older brother, but in her position she had no choice. She was virtually a prisoner in his household, and there was no means of escape. Her only hope to elude Rumbridge's authority, she realized, was marriage. Perhaps, she reflected, she should marry Milford. It would get her out of her brother's house; but that was a very sorry reason for marriage. Indeed, Georgina was hard pressed to think of anything worse than marriage to the arrogant Viscount Milford.

She was well acquainted with the viscount. He was quite handsome and a great success in society. A man of fashion and a sporting gentleman of the first order, he was viewed as an excellent catch by scores of society matrons in search of husbands for their daughters. Georgina could not abide him. He was so convinced of his own importance and ability to charm the fair sex that he failed to recognize the possibility that she was not enamoured of him. Perhaps this was because few women were immune to Milford's charm. His paramours included a bored duchess as well as several respectable married ladies and a string of less respectable women known to society as "high flyers."

Her thoughts then returned to the stranger she had met the day before, and once again she was exasperated with herself for thinking about the man. To let her thoughts dwell on some ill-mannered footman was ridiculous. But try as she might, she could not forget the young man's broad shoulders and insolent gaze. "Oh, blast the fellow!" she cried, and again determined not to waste another thought on him.

After making this resolution, Georgina rang for Sally and was soon dressed and eager to be off to her cousin's house. She knew that Rumbridge would forbid her to see Penelope that day and that her only hope was to get out of the house before seeing him or her sister-in-law. As she hurried down the stairs, she looked around; fortunately, there was no one in sight. Georgina had scribbled a hasty note in her room saying she would be spending the day at Penelope's. She placed the note on the mantel and left the house unnoticed.

When Georgina arrived at the Amesbury house, she waited at the door for some minutes before a burly, red-faced servant appeared.

"Good morning, m'lady," said the man, nodding. "Sorry to keep your ladyship waiting, but there was such a commotion I didn't hear the door."

Georgina smiled. Commotions were common in her cousin's disorganized household, but she was still curious. "Commotion, Hemmings?"

"Yes, m'lady. Mr. Ritchie and Mrs. Terrell were rehearsing a scene from a new play—and a noisy one it is, what with Mr. Ritchie shouting and Mrs. Terrell weeping and carrying on."

"I see," said Georgina. She stopped and listened. "It seems quiet now, Hemmings."

"Oh yes, m'lady. After Mr. Ritchie killed Mrs. Terrell, it got considerable quiet." Not wanting to be misunderstood, the butler quickly added. "I mean in the play, m'lady. He killed her in the play they were rehearsing."

Georgina laughed. "I am relieved to hear that! No, you don't need to announce me, Hemmings. I know my way."

Georgina quickly made her way to her cousin's sitting room. It was Penelope's favorite room, furnished in the Oriental style so admired by the Prince Regent, and she always entertained her guests there. As Georgina entered, she immediately spied her cousin standing in the center of the room. She was clad in a flowing white dress in the style of classical Greece, and her blond hair was festooned with numerous small white flowers. She stood very still, one hand poised in front of her, and her lovely eyes gazed forlornly off into the distance. At Georgina's entrance Penelope's expression abruptly changed, and she turned to her cousin with a smile.

"Georgie! How good of you to come."

At the same time there was a cry from the corner of the room, and Georgina looked over to where a thin, rabbit-faced young man stood before an easel.

"Miss Amesbury!" the man whined in exasperation. "You must not move! How can I paint you when you move about so?"

"Really, Leonard," replied Penelope in her languid voice, "I can't stand here like stone all day. If you prefer to paint a statue, go to the park. There are plenty of subjects for you there, and they shan't budge an inch."

Leonard Falconrest looked at Penelope with such a persecuted expression that Georgina almost burst into laughter. "Please, Miss Amesbury, don't say such a thing. It is you who I wish to paint, who I *must* paint!" He said these last words with feverish anxiety, and Penelope smiled.

"Oh, very well. But don't be such a tyrant, Leonard." She again turned to Georgina. "And what do you think of my pose, cousin? Tragical, is it not?"

"She is the Helen of our age," proclaimed the painter, waving his paintbrush in the air. "Such beauty is an artist's dream! Yes, she is the new Helen!"

" 'And, as befits another Helen, fired another Troy,' " boomed a voice that added, after a low, melodious chuckle, "Or at least fired up Falconrest here!"

Georgina smiled at the tall, strapping man who spoke the words. Even though he was advancing into middle age, Kenneth Ritchie was still an extremely handsome man. Women by the score had fallen in love with Ritchie's rugged good looks and beautiful baritone voice, and he continued to be one of the most popular actors of the day.

This giant of the stage had been sitting on one of Penelope Amesbury's brightly colored sofas near a flamboyantly red-haired woman and a plump, white-haired gentleman. Both gentlemen had stood up quickly when Georgina came in, but she had motioned them to sit again.

"I say," said the older gentleman with a rather idiotic grin, "I am dashed fond of beauty myself, and I'm no artist! Damn and here I find myself now, surrounded by three beautiful women." He looked at Georgina appreciatively and winked at her. Georgina winked in return, and the elderly man laughed and slapped his knee. Georgina was fond of Sir Swithin Baxter despite the fact that the elderly gentleman was not considered at all respectable. He was very wealthy and had a reputation as a notorious rake. In his younger days he had been the terror of society, and it was often said that no female was safe from him. Even at the advanced age of seventy-two, his bold eye and salty tongue made many a maiden blush, but Georgina found him somehow endearing and was one of his greatest friends.

"Sir Swithin, how well you look," she said.

"Well, damn me, girl, you are a sweet liar. You're dashed fetching today. By all the gods, if I were only five years younger."

"Five," said Penelope. "My dear Swithin, you are an optimist."

They all laughed, and Sir Swithin shook his finger at Penelope. "You bold minx," he shouted. "Come over here and I'll teach you a lesson."

Penelope smiled and returned to her pose. "Swithin, you are awful," she said. "But dear Georgie, I am so glad you are here."

"And how good it is to see you all," said Georgina, sitting down beside Sir Swithin, "although I am disappointed that I missed seeing you rehearse your new play. Hemmings seemed quite impressed by it." She turned to the red-haired lady with great interest. "And I believe you are the unfortunate murdered lady?"

The lady laughed musically, and Penelope said, "Oh dear, my manners are shocking. Georgina, this is Mrs.

Terrell. She is a quite astonishing actress who has joined Kenneth's company. Fanny, this is my cousin, Lady Georgina Suttondale."

As the two ladies exchanged pleasantries, Georgina reflected that Fanny Terrell, whether or not she was an astonishing actress, was an astonishing-looking woman. She was of indeterminate age, and her hair was a shocking shade of red. Her lips were painted a similar color, and she had lovely hazel eyes and a cream-colored complexion enhanced with a touch of rouge. She was dressed in a tight green morning dress that revealed a generously rounded figure. Georgina decided that while Mrs. Terrell might not be very well accepted by fastidious society patronesses, she would certainly be popular with their husbands.

"I do look forward to seeing this new play," said Georgina, smiling at the actress.

"Oh, it is wonderful," said Mrs. Terrell in a well-coached voice that betrayed only a hint of her lower-class origins. "And Mr. Ritchie is so very good in it," she continued, looking admiringly at her fellow actor.

"Naturally," said Ritchie, with an immodest grin. "And I do enjoy murdering you, my girl. Never have I strangled a more exquisite neck."

"I rather enjoy that part, too," said Mrs. Terrell, smiling at Ritchie, a bold look in her eyes.

"Oh, how I should like to be an actor," sighed Sir Swithin Baxter, "if *I* could put my hands around Mrs. Terrell's pretty neck."

"Oh, Sir Swithin," chided Georgina, and he patted her hand fondly.

"And do you think, Swithin, that you could become a success on the stage?" inquired Penelope.

"Certainly," said Swithin. "Why, look at Ritchie here. We're not very different, he and I. And he has the women all swooning over him. How I should love that!" And he reached over and patted Fanny Terrell playfully on the knee.

"You are incorrigible, Swithin," said Penelope with an indulgent smile.

Swithin nodded. "Just what my late wife always said. Of course," he added, somewhat regretfully, "I ain't as incorrigible as I would like to be," and he looked over at Georgina and winked again.

"Please!" came a cry, and they all turned to see Leonard Falconrest staring beseechingly at Penelope Amesbury. "You must not move, my dear Miss Amesbury." He hurried over and with one hand gently pushed her chin up a fraction of an inch. "There," he said, standing back and observing her with a smile. "That is perfect. Now don't move."

"Really, Leonard," said Penelope, but at the artist's pathetic glance she sighed and stood still.

Swithin Baxter turned his attentive gaze back to Georgina. "And how are you this fine day, Georgina? Egad, you're a good-looking girl."

"Stuff and nonsense, Swithin, and I must confess I am not in the best of moods today."

"Oh dear," said Penelope, who risked Falconrest's displeasure to look over at her cousin. "What is wrong, coz?"

"Oh, it's Rumbridge. He's so unreasonable sometimes."

"Rumbridge?" asked Mrs. Terrell.

"My cousin," explained Penelope, frowning. "The Earl of Rumbridge. He's Georgina's brother. Poor Georgie. What did Rummy say?"

"Oh, he said a lot. For one thing, he doesn't approve of me dashing about town in your phaeton. Most unladylike. He said no gentleman would ever want to marry me."

"Blast Rumbridge. I'll marry you, my girl!" blurted out Swithin, and Georgina laughed.

"Be very careful, Sir Swithin," she said, "There are witnessess here and I may very well accept your offer."

"Good," cried Sir Swithin. "It's time I had another wife."

"Yes indeed, Georgina," laughed Penelope. "You should marry Swithin. Rumbridge would be thrilled, would he not?"

"Never did like your brother," muttered Sir Swithin.

"No one does," said Penelope. "I certainly do not. He disapproves of me, you see. Always has. And of course he disapproves of Victor and all of my friends."

"Is there anyone the earl does approve of?" asked Fanny Terrell with a slight smile.

Georgina nodded. "Oh, yes. He most heartily approves of Lord Milford. He wants me to marry him!"

"Milford!" cried Penelope. "Good heavens!" She forgot about her pose and looked over at her cousin in amazement. Mr. Falconrest threw up his hands in dismay and stood pouting at his canvas.

"Milford," said Sir Swithin Baxter in disgust. "That high and mighty Milford? Can't tolerate the fellow. You ain't going to marry him over me, are you?"

"Dear me, Swithin, his lordship hasn't made me an offer. I believe it is just wishful thinking on my brother's part."

"I don't know, Georgie," said Penelope, who now wore a thoughtful expression. "Milford certainly had his eye on you at the Singletons' party. Perhaps he said something to Rumbridge."

"Oh, dear, I hope not," said Georgina.

"But Lady Georgina," said Ritchie with a broad smile, "I hear Milford is a most eligible fellow. Handsome, good family, and quite well off, too."

"Please, Mr. Ritchie, you sound like my brother. Really, it is too absurd, but Rumbridge thinks Milford the perfect husband for me, and he is fearful that I shall want to marry someone unsuitable. Rumbridge, you see, is the worst snob in the kingdom."

"Oh, I shouldn't say the worst," said Penelope. "I think Gilbert Thorpe, the renowned Viscount Milford, has that honor."

Georgina laughed. "They are a pair, aren't they? Do you know what Rumbridge said? He said he can always tell a person's birth. 'Breeding always tells,' quoth Rumbridge, and no amount of polish can hide a person's low birth."

"How utterly ridiculous!" cried Penelope. "Look at Lord Falwell. From one of the oldest families in all of England. Yet Falwell is one of the most vulgar, ill-mannered boors I have ever met. And there are a number I could name like him."

"Yes," agreed Georgina, becoming quite animated. "And some of the most polished and well-mannered gentlemen in society are not men of rank or lofty birth. I daresay Rumbridge's brag could be easily deflated. Why, I wager that I could convince him that even a footman was a prince of the blood!"

"What an intriguing idea," said Sir Swithin Baxter with his usual grin. "Even a footman, you say?"

"Yes," declared Georgina, "I daresay I could."

Penelope also seemed intrigued by the idea. "I don't know, cousin. Some footmen, perhaps; but you certainly couldn't turn that ruffian we met yesterday into a proper gentleman."

"Ruffian? What's this about a ruffian?" asked Swithin Baxter.

"Oh, you should see the fellow, Swithin. A rough rogue —looked a highwayman, didn't he, coz? He shouted at us in the street. Didn't approve of Georgina's driving; can you imagine? And the astonishing thing was, he turned out to be a servant to my own Victor. Vic must have just hired him, because I've never seen the fellow before. But I really don't think you could ever pass that one off as a gentleman."

"Well," shrugged Georgina, "I admit it would be a challenge."

"Then you think you could?" pressed Baxter.

"I could," said Georgina with more confidence than she felt.

"You are a stubborn female," replied Sir Swithin Baxter, gleefully slapping his knee. "I'll wager you can't do it."

"You'll what?"

"I'll wager you can't pass the fellow off as a gentleman to Rumbridge."

"Oh, this will be famous!" cried Penelope, suddenly excited.

"Really, cousin," said Georgina, "I don't think . . ."

"Ah, so you *don't* think you can do it, my girl?" said Sir Swithin, still grinning idiotically at her.

"No, it's just . . ."

"Oh come, Georgie," cried Penelope. "It will be a lark." She looked at Sir Swithin. "What will you wager?"

"Three hundred pounds."

"This is ridiculous," began Georgina.

"Done!" cried Penelope.

"Good!" said Swithin. "It's a wager then."

"We must set the conditions," said Penelope in a businesslike voice.

"Yes, of course, the conditions." Swithin pondered for a moment. "I've got it. I say that you must present the fellow at Lady Carrington's ball."

"Lady Carrington's ball!" cried Georgina. "That's only two weeks away."

"So it is, my dear," chuckled Sir Swithin. "You've got much work to do. The wager will rest on whether Rumbridge thinks the fellow a proper gentleman. Agreed?"

"Agreed!" cried Penelope.

"Do stop a moment," said Georgina, "I don't think . . ."

"Oh, Georgie, don't be a stick about it. You said you could do it. Perhaps two weeks is not very long, but it is more challenging, to be sure! And we two shall get Vic to help us. And, Kenneth, you and Fanny could help, too."

Ritchie smiled and bowed. "Of course, madam. I shall be happy to help."

"I will, too," said Mrs. Terrell.

Georgina looked at the faces about her and finally gave in. "All right, I shall do it. And I'll win, too!"

"Good," came a desperate voice from the corner of the room, and they all looked at a haggard Leonard Falconrest. "Now that that's all setled, may I please continue my painting? Please, Miss Amesbury?"

Penelope frowned. "Oh dear, Leonard, you can be a pest sometimes. But I'm afraid I don't have any more time right now. Georgina and I must see Victor right away." She turned back to Georgina. "I'll change, and then we'll go, cousin." She hurried out of the room, leaving an inconsolable Leonard Falconrest to lament about the whims of great ladies.

3

VICTOR BALLANVILLE SAT IN HIS DRESSING gown, sipping his morning tea. His cousin had not yet risen, surely an unusual occurrence, since Renwick was used to keeping country hours. Indeed, at Ballanville Castle it was unusual for the marquis to sleep past dawn. Victor smiled, thinking that his cousin Hugh had scarcely been in London a day, and already he was developing bad habits. The duke would not approve at all. As Mr. Ballanville sat reflecting on his cousin and his eccentric uncle, his solitude was shattered by the appearance of his fiancée and her cousin.

Penelope Amesbury, looking extremely beautiful and very determined, briskly strode into the room. She was followed by a strangely reluctant Lady Georgina Suttondale and Mrs. Grove, a dour middle-aged lady who stared glumly about the room. Most gentlemen would have been astounded by the unannounced female invasion, but Victor Ballanville smiled and greeted them in a nonchalant manner.

"Penelope, darling," he said, rising to give her a quick kiss. "And Georgina, and of course, Mrs. Grove." Mrs. Grove nodded grimly at him, and as usual Victor Ballanville found himself thinking that Mrs. Grove was an odd companion for his lively fiancée. Georgina smiled, but had no time to return his greeting, for Penelope quickly pushed him toward a chair and began talking.

"Vic, you must help us! Of course I know you will. It shall be great fun! Swithin is an idiot, but he can come up with the most amusing ideas. Oh dear, can you imagine old

Rummy's face when he finds out?" And she began laughing.

Victor Ballanville seemed not at all perturbed by this incoherent speech.

"Penelope, my dear, I shall be happy to help; but what, pray, are you talking about?"

Penelope smiled conspiratorially at Georgina and then back at Victor. "Well, you see, old dear, we made a wager with Swithin."

Victor smiled. "Knowing Swithin, my dear, I hate to imagine what the stakes are. But do go on. What is the wager?"

"Oh, it is so vastly amusing, Vic. Georgina was saying how Rumbridge was boasting how he could tell anyone's pedigree. He said no amount of polish could disguise a person's low birth. We said that was nonsense, of course, and Georgie said she bet she could even convince Rumbridge that a footman had royal blood in his veins."

"Oh?" asked Victor, looking at Georgina.

"Yes, I did say that," said Georgina with a rueful smile.

"And so," continued Penelope, "Swithin wagered that Georgina couldn't, and naturally we accepted the challenge."

"Naturally," murmured Georgina.

"So you see, Vic, we plan to turn a servant into a proper gentleman, one that would meet with even Rumbridge's approval."

Victor grinned. "Well, I wish you luck, my sweet, but how do I figure in this farce?"

"You, Victor, must lend us your servant."

"My servant?" cried Ballanville, at last showing a trace of surprise. "Smallbone?"

Penelope laughed. "Don't look so alarmed. We shan't take your precious Smallbone. It's that other fellow we want."

"Other fellow?" Victor was genuinely confused.

"The rough-looking fellow. Really, my dear, I can't imagine why you hired him, but that doesn't matter. He shall suit our purposes admirably."

"You can't mean . . . ?" began Victor in astonishment.

Suddenly, Hugh Ballanville, Marquis of Renwick, strode into the room, and Penelope let out a cry of triumph.

"There he is! That fellow!" Renwick stopped dead and stared at his cousin and the three visitors.

"That fellow . . ." echoed Victor. "But, Penelope, that 'fellow' is—"

However, his fiancée did not let him continue. "As I said, Vic, I don't know how you could hire such a ruffian." She took a critical look at Renwick. "He does look a little more presentable today." The marquis did, in fact, look much more presentable. Although his clothes were still rather shabby and old fashioned, he had shaved, and his unruly black hair had been combed into some semblance of order. After looking him over from head to toe, Penelope continued. "Still, it will be quite a challenge convincing Rumbridge that he's at all respectable, won't it, coz?"

Georgina had remained silent, but she managed to smile gamely. She then stole a glance at her adversary of the day before. He was standing at the doorway watching her, and she found herself blushing from his direct and, to her mind, impudent gaze.

Penelope, unlike her cousin, was not at all affected by the stranger's presence. She gave him another critical look and nodded her head. "Yes, he'll be a challenge all right, but that will make it so much more fun, won't it? I say, the fellow's perfect. Don't you agree, Georgie?"

Georgina nodded. "Yes, he's perfect," she said with an ironic smile.

"Thank you, m'lady," said the stranger. He made a mocking bow, and Penelope laughed.

"You see, Vic? An insolent rogue, isn't he?"

Victor shook his head. "I really must explain, Penelope. This is somewhat embarrassing, but I must tell you that this is . . ."

However, this time he was interrupted by his cousin. "I'll not be ridiculed, Mr. Ballanville. I'll give my notice," said Renwick in a sullen voice, exaggerating his north country accent and fixing mischievous blue eyes on his cousin. Victor Ballanville, who was quite familiar with that look, fought back a smile. He and his cousin Hugh had played many a prank together as youngsters, and Victor had learned to quickly take his cousin's lead.

He frowned at Renwick. "I shouldn't be too hasty in giving your notice, my man. Not many would hire you." He turned apologetically to Penelope and Georgina. "As you say, the fellow is insolent. I only took him on as a favor to Smallbone."

"Smallbone?" said Penelope, raising her eyebrows in surprise.

"Yes, he's Smallbone's nephew." He lowered his voice and leaned closer to the ladies. "Smallbone's sister's son. The fellow's been a trial to his poor mother. From up north, they are. Always getting himself into scrapes, as you can imagine from the look of him."

Georgina glanced over at Smallbone's incorrigible nephew and found him leaning back against the doorway, his arms folded in front of him. He met her gaze with a sudden devilish grin, and she frowned.

"This is all rather surprising," Penelope was saying. "Smallbone's nephew?"

"Yes, poor Smallbone."

"Well, Vic, it is of no matter," said Penelope. "As I said, he shall suit our purposes admirably."

"Beggin' your pardon, miss," said Renwick, "but what might those purposes be?"

"You, my good man," said Penelope, "are to help us win a wager."

"Me, miss?"

"Yes. I wagered that Lady Georgina could pass you off to her brother as a proper gentleman."

Renwick looked curiously at Georgina. "Me, a gentleman? Bloody unlikely."

"Watch your tongue, man," cried Victor Ballanville, trying hard not to laugh. "Damned if I shouldn't take a horsewhip to you!"

Renwick himself almost burst into laughter at his cousin's ludicrous outrage, but instead he muttered, in an unrepentant voice, "Beggin' your pardon, Mr. Ballanville. M'lady. I was forgettin' myself."

"Now, Victor," said Penelope, "you mustn't let him upset you so. After all, a person of his station is not accustomed to speaking to ladies, and he *is* going to help us with our bet."

"If I may be so bold, miss," said Renwick.

"Yes?" asked Penelope.

"Before I'd be helping you ladies, I'd like to know what's in it for me."

"Rascal!" said Victor threateningly. "Smallbone or no, I'll send you on your way."

"No, Victor, you can't do that," said Georgina firmly, and they all looked at her in surprise. She stood up and resolutely walked over to stand directly in front of Renwick. Renwick found to his surprise that he was somewhat disconcerted by the lady's dark gaze and frank speech.

"I daresay you dislike me as much as I dislike you, but I do need your help. I assure you, you'll be well paid for your trouble. Would twenty-five pounds suffice?"

He smiled back at her. "Aye, twenty-five pounds is more'n I'm likely to see in a year, m'lady."

The man continued to smile at her, and Georgina felt herself blushing. "I do not even know your name," she said, doing her best to sound nonchalant.

"That's right," cried Penelope. "What is your name, my good man?"

Renwick paused for just a moment, and then smiled as he thought of the name of his father's rough-hewn valet. "Sam Botts at your service," he said, bowing.

Victor Ballanville, who was well acquainted with the original Sam Botts, burst into laughter at this announcement, but quickly attempted to disguise it in a fit of coughing.

Penelope cast her fiancé a strange look, but then turned back to Renwick.

"Sam Botts?" And she wrinkled her nose as if she had just caught whiff of a most unpleasant smell. "Well, Sam Botts is hardly a gentleman's name. We must change that name with all due haste." Georgina almost laughed at the offended expression on Botts's face. Penelope, however, ignored this and looked him over thoughtfully. "Let's see. We must give you a new identity. Hmmmm. . . ." Her face took on a look of strained concentration, and Victor laughed. Then, suddenly, he had an inspiration, and he grinned.

"Penelope, darling, don't look so perplexed. Since I should love nothing better than to see old Swithin lose a bit of his blunt, I will help you. In fact, I have the perfect solution for Sam here."

"You do?" His fiancée sounded skeptical.

"Yes," said Victor triumphantly. "We'll pass the fellow off as my cousin Hugh."

This time it was Renwick's turn to hold back his laughter, and he did so with great effort.

"Your cousin Hugh?" asked Penelope incredulously. "Do you mean the Marquis of Renwick? Son of the Duke of Welham?"

"Of course, my dear."

Penelope and Georgina both burst out laughing. "Really, Vic," said Penelope. "You are an ambitious fellow. Passing off Sam as the heir to a dukedom?"

Victor smiled slyly at his cousin. "I know it seems an impossible feat, but really it is perfect. My cousin Hugh lives up in the barbaric northlands and never comes down to London. A dreadful provincial, my cousin Hugh."

Penelope became thoughtful again. "That is true. Vic has told me all about his cousin and his eccentric uncle. I suppose it would explain his quaint accent and some of his rough edges. But really, Vic, I don't know. A marquis, after all! Perhaps it is a bit too high. Surely a second son of a baronet might sound more convincing."

Georgina nodded in agreement. "You really can't be serious, Victor."

"So, m'lady," said Renwick, frowning disapprovingly at her. "You ain't so sure of yourself, after all, are you?"

Georgina sighed in exasperation. "I am sure of myself, but it is you, Sam Botts, I have little faith in. Do you think you could do it? Pass yourself off as the Marquis of Renwick in two weeks' time?"

He suddenly grinned at her. "For twenty-five pounds, m'lady, I could be the Prince Regent himself."

She looked at him for a moment and then laughed. "All right, then, Sam Botts, you are now the Marquis of Renwick."

Penelope smiled. "My dears, I think the fellow can do it."

"Yes," observed Victor dryly, "why Botts even is beginning to look a little like my cousin Hugh."

"A handsome fellow, is he?" said Renwick, still grinning. Penelope and Victor laughed, but Georgina frowned at his audacity and reflected that Sam Botts did not have sufficient respect for his betters.

At that moment Smallbone entered the room, and Penelope Amesbury smiled at him. "Oh, Smallbone, you will be glad to know your nephew Sam has become engaged in a rather profitable enterprise."

"My nephew *Sam,* Miss?" asked Smallbone, gaping at her. Jimmy Smallbone had a number of nephews, but none was christened Sam. Renwick smiled and patted Smallbone affectionately on the shoulder.

"Yes, Uncle . . ." He hesitated, and found he did not know the worthy servant's first name. "I shall tell you all about it later." He winked at Smallbone, and the servant looked even more confused.

"Smallbone, I think some tea for the ladies would be in order."

"Yes, sir," said Smallbone, who was grateful to leave the room.

Penelope Amesbury did not notice Smallbone's confusion, for she was still studying Renwick with a thoughtful expression. "I think the first thing to be done is to get Sam to your tailor. You can see to that, can't you, Vic?"

"Yes, my dear," said Victor, grinning at his cousin, who did not seem at all daunted by the lady's critical gaze.

"But if you'll excuse me a minute, my love," said Victor, "I have to talk to Sam in private about something." He pointed toward the doorway, and his cousin obligingly stepped out into the hallway.

"Listen, Hugh," whispered Victor, "this has all been rather jolly, but don't you think it's gone far enough?"

Renwick grinned. "What's wrong, Vic? Don't you want to share your tailor with me?"

Victor smiled. "Come now, cousin, I am being serious."

"Don't worry, Victor, I shan't carry it too far," said Renwick, his eyes full of devilment. "But do go along with it a bit longer, won't you?"

Ballanville hesitated. "All right, cousin. I confess it is a great joke. Egad, Sam Botts!" and he began to laugh.

"Steady, Vic," said Renwick, glancing back toward the room. Victor composed himself and nodded.

When the two men returned, Penelope and Georgina were busy discussing future plans. Mrs. Grove, who did not really approve of the enterprise, but did not care enough to say so, sat there with a sullen expression on her face.

"And we will get Kenneth and Fanny to help with his

speech and manners," Penelope was saying. She looked up as Victor and Renwick reentered the room. "Oh, Vic, after you get Sam to your tailor, you must bring him over to my house. How about tomorrow afternoon?"

"All right, darling."

She stood up, and Georgina rose to follow her. "Georgie and I will go now so you two can see your tailor right away. We do not have much time, and Sam does need a lot of work."

"Sam" smiled. "I be a fast learner, miss."

"I daresay," murmured Lady Georgina sarcastically, and as she looked at him, she felt definite misgivings about the venture. There was something about the man that unsettled her. Perhaps it was those impudent blue eyes of his. As she reflected on this, he turned those disquieting eyes toward her and smiled. Georgina looked away quickly. "We should be off then, Victor. Good day to you." She hesitated, and looked over at Renwick. He grinned at her, and, grasping Penelope's arm, she quickly propelled her cousin out the door, with Mrs. Grove following close behind.

4

WHEN GEORGINA RETURNED LATER THAT AFternoon, she was met by an apologetic-looking Tabb. The butler smiled at her, but Georgina could tell he had some unpleasant news.

"Hello, Tabb, is something the matter?"

"No, my lady. Only Lord Rumbridge said to inform your ladyship that he wants to see you as soon as you come in."

Georgina sighed. "Not in the library again?"

Tabb smiled slightly. "No, Lady Georgina. His lordship and Lady Rumbridge are in the sitting room. They are waiting tea for you."

"Heavens, they could have tea without me! But do not fear, Tabb, you can tell them that I will join them shortly." And she hurried up to her room to change her dress.

A few moments later Georgina, clad in a light green dress that complemented her dark looks, ran down the hall toward the sitting room and almost collided with Tabb in the doorway.

"My lady," said the butler in some astonishment, "I just told them you would be down shortly."

Georgina laughed. "Well, this is shortly, isn't it, Tabb?"

The butler smiled, and she proceeded past him into the room. She noted her brother standing by the mantel, still looking extremely displeased with her, but she smiled brightly at him.

"Robert, you should not have waited tea on me." Without waiting for a reply, she greeted her sister-in-law and sat down on the sofa.

"And where have you been, miss?" asked the earl testily.

Georgina looked at him in wide-eyed innocence. "Why, Robert, whatever is the matter? I know you like your tea punctually at four o'clock, but really, you did not have to wait for—"

"Blast my punctual tea, Georgina! Where have you been?"

"I've been to Penelope's. I left you a note." She looked at the mantel behind him. "Oh, dear, there it is. You didn't see it?"

The earl glared at the note and then at his sister. The countess also regarded Georgina with disapproval.

"Really, Georgina," she said, "you shouldn't leave notes about the house. And you should not be going off without even a 'good morning' to us. It is not done. What is anyone to think of you going off in such a manner unescorted?"

Georgina frowned. "I had promised Penelope I would come early, and I didn't want to disturb anyone. But I promise in the future I shall announce my departure with all due fanfare."

"There is no call to be impudent, my girl," said the Earl of Rumbridge sternly. "And so you were gallivanting around town with Penelope again. I suspected as much. And after our talk yesterday. I might have known you would ignore my wishes."

"Oh please, Rumbridge, we were not 'gallivanting' about town. Indeed, we had a very quiet, uneventful day together."

"A quiet and uneventful day in the company of Miss Amesbury?" remarked Lady Rumbridge archly. "That is impossible!"

Georgina managed a smile. "I must confess, Amelia, my cousin's house is never dull."

Lady Rumbridge and her husband exchanged glances and frowned.

"And how did you happen to get over to Penelope's house, Georgina?" continued her brother. "You didn't have any of the servants take you. I suppose Penelope had someone come for you in that blasted phaeton of hers."

"Oh no, Robert. I know you said you disapprove of me

riding about in Penelope's phaeton. I walked over to her house."

"You what?"

"I walked. I needed the exercise."

"Walked unescorted?" gasped the countess.

"Yes, but it is not far, as you well know."

"Have you no sensibility at all?" shouted her brother angrily. "Walking about the streets alone?"

"But it is just a few blocks," protested Georgina.

"A few blocks!" said Rumbridge. "Well, my girl, you shall not be taking this little walk again, I promise you. I forbid you to visit your cousin again without my permission." The countess nodded in approval and continued to scold her for her shocking behavior. Georgina listened for a time in indignant and unrepentant silence.

Finally, she could take no more of their recriminations and, rising abruptly, bade them good afternoon. Rumbridge called her back, but she ignored him and retreated to her room. Once inside, she threw herself upon her bed and hid her face in her pillow.

Georgina did not enjoy spending so much time sulking in her room, and yet she had no wish to see her sister-in-law or brother any more that day. Her response to her brother's summons for dinner that evening was another polite message that she was indisposed; and although Rumbridge was irritated, he vowed she might stay there as long as she wished. Reflecting that life was hard indeed, Georgina spent the evening in her sitting room, eating a simple supper brought up by her faithful Sally and reading a novel.

In the morning, however, Georgina awoke with a resolve to try anew to get back into Rumbridge's good graces. It was the only course open to her, for the earl could, if he so desired, prevent her from seeing Penelope or anyone else. It was barbarous that one's brother could so control one's life even at the age of twenty-two, she thought, but she would try to make the best of it.

After pondering her situation, Georgina instructed Sally to lay out a very plain and modest blue morning dress, a dress she detested but one that her sister-in-law thought quite acceptable. She dressed carefully and went downstairs, where she found her brother and the countess preparing for breakfast. Both of them greeted her with distant nods, and Georgina sat down at the table, wondering how best to placate these difficult people.

Remaining discreetly silent at breakfast, Georgina thought she could detect Rumbridge softening a bit toward her. She thought it possible to chance some conversation and made an innocuous comment about the weather. Rumbridge responded in a quite civil manner, and Georgina was emboldened to direct an inquiry to the countess about the health of her two sons, who were away at school.

Since Lady Rumbridge liked nothing better than to discuss her sons and, by fortunate coincidence, had just received a letter from her eldest son, the twelve-year-old Viscount Hadly, the countess began to relate the letter's contents in great detail. Encouraged by her success, Georgina decided to do her best to give her sister-in-law no cause that day for further disapproval.

This was not altogether easy; for, later that day when they were all sitting together, the ladies engaged in needlework and the earl sitting amiably with them, the countess asked about her cousin Penelope.

"And so, Georgina," said Lady Rumbridge coolly, "how is Miss Amesbury?"

Georgina ignored her sister-in-law's disagreeable tone and added a stitch to her canvas. "Oh, she is very well. She's having her portrait painted."

"Good lord," said the earl, "the girl's always getting her portrait painted by some fool. What fellow is painting her this time?"

"Leonard Falconrest. A brilliant artist, by his own estimation, and quite the rage in town this season. Actually, he is quite good, but you should see how he worships Cousin Penelope. It is quite funny."

"Indeed?" sniffed the countess, and she shook her head. "Of course, one must be careful not to encourage such admiration from inferiors. It can be rather embarrassing."

"Do not worry, Amelia," said Georgina. "Penelope is not at all encouraging to Mr. Falconrest. Indeed, she is quite the opposite; poor man."

"I am sure 'poor' Mr. Falconrest was not the only one at your cousin's house," said the earl.

"Oh no. Mr. Kenneth Ritchie and a Mrs. Terrell were there, and of course Mrs. Grove." Georgina discreetly omitted mention of Sir Swithin Baxter or the fact that Mrs. Grove had spent most of the morning in her room.

"Actors," muttered Rumbridge.

"Dear me," said the countess.

"But I assure you they both were quite nice and very pleasant."

Rumbridge frowned. "That cousin of mine always has the most unsuitable persons at her house. As I said before, Georgina, you should be more careful of the company you keep."

Georgina stopped herself with some difficulty from blurting out a rude remark. Instead, she nodded meekly.

"Indeed," said Lady Rumbridge. "It is very well to see these actors on stage, but one does not invite them to one's house."

Rumbridge nodded, and although Georgina was becoming dangerously irritated, she managed to change the subject.

"I also saw Victor Ballanville yesterday," she said, and a mischievous gleam suddenly appeared in her eyes. "Did you know Victor's cousin is coming to town for a visit?"

"One of his mother's family, I presume?" inquired the earl disdainfully. Although Victor Ballanville's maternal relations were, for the most part, respectable enough, it was a well-known fact that his mother's family was impoverished.

"Oh no," replied Georgina with a sly smile. "Not one of the Marshfields. This cousin is a Ballanville."

"A Ballanville?" asked Lady Rumbridge, suddenly leaning forward and looking at her sister-in-law with great interest.

"Yes. Hugh Ballanville, the Marquis of Renwick. He is son of the Duke of Welham."

"Of course!" said Lady Rumbridge. "The Duke of Welham. Lives up north and is quite wealthy, so they say. But he is somewhat mysterious. He and his family never venture down to London."

"Well," replied Georgina, "apparently Victor's cousin has finally decided to come to the wicked city."

"And is this Renwick married yet?"

"No, or I do not think so."

Lady Rumbridge looked calculatingly at Georgina and then turned to her husband. The countess was even more eager than her husband to see Georgina married, and the mention of any eligible man sparked her interest. However, the earl did not seem aware of the importance of this news, and she gave an exasperated sigh. She turned back to Georgina and smiled for the first time. The countess did not smile very often, and Georgina reflected it did not at all suit her, giving her face a curious look of insincerity and reminding Georgina of a fox staring into a chicken coop.

"Georgina, my dear, this is extremely lucky for you. You must not let such an opportunity pass by."

"What opportunity, Amelia?"

"Why, to snare a prize like the Marquis of Renwick, the heir to a dukedom!"

Georgina laughed. "But Amelia, I don't even know the marquis."

"That is of no matter, Georgina," said Lady Rumbridge quickly. "You will meet him, to be sure. After all, you are Penelope's cousin, and she is engaged to Mr. Ballanville. You will be at a great advantage!"

Rumbridge seemed to be weighing his wife's words, and he nodded. "Yes, Amelia is right, Georgina. This Lord Renwick sounds extremely eligible. Rich, of the highest rank."

"Oh, dear, Robert, you are fickle," said Georgina, a merry expression in her dark eyes.

"I am what?" asked her brother in surprise.

"Fickle, brother. Why you were just recently singing me the praises of Lord Milford, that pillar of *ton*. And now you toss Milford aside for Renwick, a man you do not even know. And what of poor Milford? I'm sure his lordship would be heartbroken if I so callously threw him over . . . even for a future duke. I mean, Milford is obviously so devoted to me." Having said this with a straight face, Georgina could control herself no longer, and burst out laughing. Rumbridge frowned, but before he could reply to his incorrigible young sister, Tabb came into the room.

"The Viscount of Milford is here, my lord."

"Milford?" said Georgina in surprise. "Oh dear, perhaps he has already heard about his rival and is here to press his suit."

Rumbridge's frown grew deeper. "I warn you, Georgina, quit this nonsense and be sensible."

Georgina smiled. "I'm sorry, Robert. I promise I will try." But her eyes still sparkled, and her brother regarded her warily. However, he had no choice but to tell the butler to bring his lordship in.

Tabb returned shortly and solemnly announced, "The Viscount of Milford." His words were followed by the magnificent appearance of his lordship.

Lord Milford was a tall man whose elegant clothes were impeccably suited to his well-formed frame. His dark brown hair was carefully coiffed in the latest style, and his features, all save for a somewhat weak chin, were quite dashing. His lordship always wore a rather bored expression on his handsome face, and as he entered the Earl of Rumbridge's sitting room, he glanced wearily at the room's occupants. His gaze alighted on the Lady Georgina and then, after what seemed to be a quick appraisal, returned to the earl.

"Rumbridge," he announced in the haughty voice that never failed to irritate Georgina. "I hope you and the ladies do not mind this intrusion."

"Of course not, Milford," said the earl, looking sideways at his sister and being relieved to find that she was sitting meekly, her eyes downcast. He did not know that this posture of humility was due to her attempt to refrain from laughing at the pompous Milford. "We were just about to have tea," continued Rumbridge. "Please do sit down."

Milford nodded, but before sitting down, he approached the ladies. He greeted the countess with well-practiced civility and then turned to Georgina.

"Lady Georgina," he said, smiling down at her. Georgina did not like his lordship's condescending smile or the self-satisfied look in his eyes, but she held out her hand and smiled.

"And how are you this day, my lord?"

Milford took her proffered hand and, to her surprise, raised it to his lips. "I am indeed well in your ladyship's presence." He looked so sure of his charm that Georgina almost burst out laughing.

"The pompous ass," she thought, as she continued to smile at him. "Do sit down, my lord," she said, and his lordship, after surveying the room, sat down in a chair nearest to her.

His critical gaze flitted about the room for a moment and returned to Georgina. There was an awkward silence, and he smiled again in his condescending fashion. "I fear I have interrupted your conversation. Pray do continue."

Georgina looked at her brother and saw the concern on his face. She smiled back at Milford.

"I was only telling about Victor Ballanville's cousin, my lord. You know Mr. Ballanville, do you not? He is to marry my cousin Penelope."

"Of course," murmured Milford; and he wondered how anyone, even someone like Ballanville, who was no doubt in desperate financial straits, could marry that irritating Amesbury female. Milford vowed he would sever that connection once he had married the Lady Georgina.

"Yes, well," continued Georgina, "Victor's cousin is coming to London for the first time. He is from up north, you see."

"Oh dear," said Milford with a pained expression, "another provincial bumpkin descending on polite society."

His words irritated Georgina. "This 'provincial bumpkin,' as you call him, my lord, will no doubt be a great success in society."

"Really?" Milford raised his eyebrows in a bemused expression.

"Even provincial bumpkins can be a success in society if they are heirs to dukedoms."

The Earl of Rumbridge did not like the challenge in his sister's voice and frowned disapprovingly at her. Lord Milford merely smiled.

"Heir to a dukedom?"

Lady Rumbrige broke in. "Yes, the Marquis of Renwick, son of the Duke of Welham. Frightfully rich, they say."

"An extremely eligible bumpkin, wouldn't you say, my lord?" asked Georgina.

"I daresay," said Milford. "I shall have to help acquaint this eligible marquis to society."

Georgina almost laughed as she thought of Milford taking Sam Botts under his wing. "That would be very kind of you, my lord," she murmured.

Lord Milford was becoming bored by all the talk about

the Marquis of Renwick, who, despite his enviable rank, was unknown to society. He turned the discussion to his meeting with the Prince Regent the previous day.

The viscount's ill humor deserted him quickly as he talked about himself and reflected that the Lady Georgina was smitten with him. He had suspected as much, but her intent expression provided final proof. This pleased the viscount very much, for he was quite taken with the Lady Georgina. After all, he thought, she was very attractive, and she did have rank and would bring a nice-sized dowry. These were important considerations when one was looking for a wife, and the viscount had reluctantly decided it was time to marry. Although Lady Georgina's manner was rather outspoken for a female, and despite her other flaws (and Milford's discerning eye could note many), the viscount wanted Georgina and had decided after much thought to make her his wife. As he sat smiling at her, the thought never occurred to him that the Lady Georgina would not accept him.

5

THE FOLLOWING AFTERNOON LADY GEORGINA was relieved to find that Rumbridge had no objection to her calling upon her cousin Penelope. Perhaps this was because she had asked him with such uncharacteristic submissiveness that the earl believed she had learned her lesson and was willing to accept authority.

Georgina arrived at her cousin's house and, after greeting Penelope warmly, began to tell her of Milford's visit.

"Milford came to tea?" said Penelope in some surprise. "My dear coz, this does sound serious. Did he make you an offer?"

Georgina laughed. "Don't be ridiculous, Penelope. His lordship could not want to marry me! Indeed, I can't imagine him condescending to marry anyone."

Penelope smiled. "Yes, I doubt any lady would meet Milford's standard of perfection, which is, of course, himself."

Georgina laughed.

"But perhaps," continued Penelope, "his lordship has decided to do his lordly duty and set up a nursery."

"Oh dear," said Georgina, "what a distressing thought."

"Well, in any case, my dear, I do hope Rumbridge doesn't try to force this match on you."

"Don't be silly. Rumbridge could never force me to marry a fool like Milford. And I didn't tell you, but my brother has found another marriage prospect for me. An even better prospect than Milford."

Penelope looked surprised. "A better prospect than

Milford? That's difficult to imagine. Who is this eligible fellow?"

Georgina smiled. "The Marquis of Renwick."

"What?" cried Penelope.

Georgina laughed. "It was so funny, cousin. I told Rumbridge and Amelia about Victor's cousin coming to town for a visit, and they immediately decided he would be perfect for me. A future duke, after all!"

Her cousin laughed. "Oh, this is famous! Can you imagine old Rummy trying to marry you off to the eligible Marquis of Renwick only to find out he is really Sam . . . oh, what is the fellow's name?"

"Botts."

"Yes. Dreadful name. I do hope Vic brings him here soon. I asked Kenneth and Fanny to come over, and they should be here any minute." She heard the knock at the door and smiled. "Oh good, perhaps that's them now." Her smile faded as a grinning Sir Swithin Baxter entered the room.

"Swithin! What are you doing here?"

The elderly gentleman chuckled. "Not a very warm greeting, my dear." He lowered his rotund form into a chair and winked at Georgina. "Actually, I heard that Georgina's ruffian was going to be here, so I wanted to get a look at the fellow."

"Are you worried about your three hundred pounds?" asked Georgina, smiling.

"No, no, dear lady. Not worried a bit. Just curious to see your ruffian."

The butler then entered to announce the actors Kenneth Ritchie and Fanny Terrell. As Fanny Terrell entered the room, she saw the disappointed look on Swithin Baxter's face. She smiled. "You do not look happy to see us, Sir Swithin."

That gentleman's face brightened. "Nonsense, Mrs. Terrell. I'm always happy to see such a dashed pretty girl like you. I only thought you'd be Lady Georgina's ruffian. I'm damned curious to see the fellow."

"Really, Swithin," protested Georgina, "must you refer to him as 'my ruffian'?"

Swithin grinned. "Very well, my girl. What should I call the fellow?"

"'My lord,' I should think," returned Georgina, and they all laughed.

"I am glad you could come, Kenneth," said Penelope, turning to that gentleman. "I am sure you and Fanny will be a great help."

"It shall be an honor to help you ladies," replied Ritchie, bestowing upon them the same smile that had charmed countless audiences.

"I just hope," remarked Georgina, "that your pupil is not too difficult."

"What's this?" cried Swithin Baxter. "Is that *doubt* in my lady's voice? Perhaps Miss Amesbury regrets her bold wager?"

"Nonsense, Swithin," scoffed Penelope. "I already consider myself three hundred pounds richer."

At that moment the butler entered the room again and announced, "The Marquis of Renwick and Mr. Ballanville."

A smiling Victor Ballanville walked in alone and, standing to one side, waited for the marquis. When Renwick strode into the room, his appearance provoked quite a sensation. The company all gaped at him in silence until Fanny Terrell, in a lapse revealing her South London origins, exclaimed, "Oooh, but 'e's a 'andsome one, ain't 'e?" The marquis could not help but hear these words, and he looked over toward the actress and bowed.

The tailor had indeed done a remarkable job in outfitting the marquis. Renwick's coat was of impeccable cut, worthy of the Beau himself. He wore a flowing white neck cloth tied in the latest fashion, nankeen pantaloons, and a pair of gleaming Hessian boots. The outfit showed off Renwick's broad shoulders and athletic build to perfection. In addition to admiring his lordship's physique, Fanny Terrell was also thrilled by his roguish good looks, and she gave him a bold smile of approval.

The Lady Georgina saw Mrs. Terrell's smile and frowned. She, too, had been somewhat taken aback by Renwick's dashing appearance. She had to admit the fellow was good looking. No doubt he had conquered many unsuspecting female hearts with his looks, and those infernal blue eyes of his. He had them focused appreciatively on the actress now, and Georgina felt strangely irritated. Then he turned to her and grinned.

"Well, m'lady," he said in his exaggerated north country accent. "What do you think? Don't I look a nob? A right proper gent I be."

Georgina shrugged. "You look . . . presentable," she conceded grudgingly, "but you are quite far from being a proper gentleman."

Swithin Baxter, who had been somewhat worried by Renwick's lordly appearance, was quite relieved when the fellow opened his mouth. He looked from Renwick to Georgina and chuckled to himself.

Penelope was also amused. "I daresay my coz is right. You aren't a 'proper gent' yet, but you do look quite the blade, Sam." She glanced over at her fiancé and smiled. "Your tailor did an admirable job, Vic."

Victor Ballanville sat down wearily in a chair and shook his head.

"I tell you, my love, it wasn't easy. Sam here was most uncooperative with the poor man. Egad, I doubt old Watson will want my business after this."

Sam Botts looked offended. "But Mr. Ballanville, the fellow was trying to make me wear those blasted britches. They was too tight," he explained to the ladies, who looked somewhat surprised by this admission. Swithin Baxter chuckled, and a wide smile appeared on Kenneth Ritchie's face.

"I tell you the fellow was a fool," continued Renwick. "I says to him, 'I'm not wearin' those britches. I can't even move in 'em.' And *he* says, 'But, sir, 'tis the fashion.' Then he tells me some fool story about some nob client of his what's always had two pairs of britches made . . . one for sitting and one for standing. Did you ever hear such foolishness?" He looked earnestly at them all and was undeterred by their lack of response. "Well, I told the fellow I didn't give a damn about fashion and I wouldn't wear the bloody britches!"

"Really," cried Georgina, looking quite appalled. "You should not speak so in the presence of ladies."

"Yes, my man," agreed an amused Victor Ballanville. "You should save such crudity for the company of gentlemen."

Penelope laughed. "I can see, my darling, that you shall be a wonderful influence on Sam." She looked at

Georgina and smiled. "Don't you think introductions are in order, coz?"

Georgina gave a slight shrug. "I suppose so." She hesitated, and then turned to Kenneth Ritchie. "Mr. Ritchie, this is Sam Botts, or shall I say the Marquis of Renwick?" She looked disapprovingly at Renwick. "Mr. Ritchie has agreed to help us in this venture, although I daresay he has begun to have second thoughts."

Ritchie smiled with his usual charm and shook hands with the marquis. "No second thoughts, I assure you, my lady. It will be a challenge to the skills of my profession."

"And what might that profession be?" asked Renwick.

Ritchie seemed momentarily taken aback, but he quickly recovered his aplomb and smiled. "It is a profession, young man, that requires a great deal of vanity, and I fear you have been a blow to mine."

Georgina looked at Renwick and shook her head. "You mean you have never heard of Kenneth Ritchie? Why, he is one of England's finest actors."

Renwick smiled apologetically at the actor. "I do beg your pardon, sir, but where I'm from we don't see many plays. I did see one once, and a grand thing it was."

"Oh, then you must see our play," piped in Fanny Terrell.

Renwick smiled at her and turned expectantly to Georgina.

She frowned. "Mrs. Terrell, this is Sam Botts. Mrs. Terrell is an actress and will be appearing in Mr. Ritchie's theatre company."

"How do, Mrs. Terrell," said Renwick, smiling. "I should like nothing better than to see you on the stage."

"You must come, then," said Mrs. Terrell. "Indeed, sir," she murmured, smiling flirtatiously, "I shall insist upon it."

Renwick was about to reply, but was cut off from doing so by Lady Georgina. "I must also introduce Sir Swithin Baxter, who is the one betting against us."

"Nothing personal, mind you," said Swithin, nodding at the marquis with his characteristically overeager expression. "Dashed if I don't almost think the lady can do it," continued Baxter. "By God, this fellow *looks* the part well enough. But Rumbridge ain't a fool, my girl, and I do think my money is safe."

"I fear you are wrong, Swithin," said Penelope. "My cousin Rumbridge may not be a fool, but he is easily blinded by rank and title. Look at how he is trying to throw my poor coz at Milford."

"What's that?" asked Victor.

"Oh, I did not tell you, my dear, but Rumbridge wants Georgie to marry Milford."

"The devil! Milford! Can't stand the fellow. You ain't going to marry him are you, Georgina?"

Before she could reply, Penelope laughed. "Heavens, Vic, I think Georgie would rather marry Sam here than Milford."

Georgina reddened. "Really, Penelope."

"It is most amusing, my dear," continued Penelope, blithely ignoring her cousin's embarrassment, "but when Rummy heard about your illustrious cousin coming to London, he immediately seized upon him as a prospective bridegroom for Georgie. Can you imagine when he finds out that your eligible cousin is really Sam? It shall be a great joke! Oh, I am so looking forward to Lady Carrington's ball, and it's usually the dreariest event of the season."

"Right you are, my dear," said Baxter. "I don't know why no one ever misses the affair. Lady Carrington never fails to assemble the most interminable bores."

Penelope nodded. "She never fails to invite *you*, does she, Swithin?"

The gentleman seemed not at all offended by this remark, and grinned. "My dear Penelope, you will have to leave off any further insults for another time, for I must be going."

"Must you leave so soon, Swithin?"

"Yes, I fear I must."

"And I fear, Miss Amesbury," said Kenneth Ritchie, also rising to his feet, "that Mrs. Terrell and I must also be on our way."

"Yes," said Fanny, looking reluctantly at Renwick. "I suppose we must be off."

"But I shall come to Mr. Ballanville's house tomorrow afternoon," said Ritchie, "to begin Sam's lessons. Shall we say about two o'clock?"

"Splendid," said Victor.

"Oh, I shall come, too," said Mrs. Terrell eagerly. She

cast another coquettish look at Renwick, and Georgina shook her head.

"I do not think that will be necessary, Mrs. Terrell, but it is kind of you to offer to help. I know you are very busy."

Fanny Terrell was irritated at being pushed out of the picture, especially since she was looking forward to seeing more of the handsome Sam Botts. However, she decided it best not to disagree with a lady of Georgina's rank. "As you say, my lady," she said smiling. She looked over at Renwick. "I do hope to see you at our play, Sam."

"I wouldn't miss it, Mrs. Terrell," he said.

"Then afterward you must come backstage and tell me how you liked it," said Fanny with a suggestive smile.

Renwick smiled back. "I can already tell that I'll like it, ma'am. But I think I would like anything that had you on stage."

Georgina observed this conversation with a frown. She did not know why Fanny Terrell suddenly annoyed her so much, but it was most shocking to see her flirt so brazenly with a common footman. Perhaps Rumbridge was not so far wrong in his opinion of actors.

After they had left, Georgina turned her attention upon Renwick and found herself wishing he were not so attractive.

"He is grand, is he not?" said Penelope, casting another appraising look at Renwick. "Yes, Sam, Victor has you looking the part well enough, and I daresay Kenneth will soon have you acting the part. Let's see, what shall we do now? I have it! We must teach you to dance!"

"Oh, I dance very well, miss," said Renwick. "There be many dances that we do up in north country."

Penelope laughed. "Well, Sam, I doubt they will be doing those quaint dances at Lady Carrington's ball. You need to learn some modern dances." She turned to her cousin. "You can teach him, Georgie."

Georgina looked startled. "I really don't think . . ."

"Oh, don't be so modest, coz You are a wonderful dancer. Let's go to the drawing room."

Before she could protest further, Georgina found herself being led forcefully to the drawing room and thrust into the arms of Sam Botts. To her great irritation, he seemed to enjoy her discomfiture.

Penelope sat down at the pianoforte, and Victor sat beside her. She began to play in a most inept fashion, the tune barely discernible as a waltz. Georgina sighed as her cousin called over to them, "Do get started."

"She expects us to dance to *that,* m'lady?" said Renwick, a look of incredulity on his face.

Georgina frowned once again, for although she had been thinking the same thing, she thought it most inappropriate for Sam Botts to comment upon her cousin's appalling lack of musical talent. "Shall we get started, Sam? The waltz is very popular, and you must learn it."

"Waltz?" said Renwick in mock horror. "We don't waltz in my county. Folk there think it immoral. Lucifer's dance, our vicar calls it!"

"Oh heavens!" cried Georgina. "This is London, and if you fear for your virtue, Mr. Botts, let me assure you you have no cause."

Renwick laughed. "I have your word on that, m'lady?"

"Oh, you are insufferable! I don't want another word from you, Sam Botts. Watch me, now. You see, it is like this—*one,* two, three; *one,* two, three. There, you see? Try it."

Renwick nodded and made an awkward attempt at the steps.

"Oh, I can see this is going to be difficult. Here, put your arm around my waist. Good. And then take my hand. Now follow me."

Renwick, who despite his provincial background was in reality a fine dancer and a master of the daring new waltz, tried very hard to do his worst. He moved so awkwardly that Georgina was soon ready to throw up her hands in frustration. "Do try harder, Sam," cried Georgina "Concentrate." She continued to pull him along. "*One,* two, three; *one,* two, three," she repeated; but to no avail, and when his foot took the wrong step, she trod upon it.

"Ow!" he cried, stopping and looking accusingly at her. "I thought you was a *good* dancer, m'lady."

"Oh you!" cried Georgina, pulling away from him. "I am a good dancer. If you were not so clumsy!"

"But it was your ladyship what stepped on *my* foot. I do hope I ain't lamed permanent."

"I should be happy if you were lamed permanently," cried Georgina. "You are hopeless."

Penelope and Victor had been so intent upon each other that they had not been paying much attention to the dancers. But at this outburst, Penelope stopped playing.

"Whatever is the matter with you two?"

"It is hopeless, Penelope. He is so awkward. I doubt he could ever learn. I think we were mad to accept the wager."

Victor nodded and cast a quizzical look at Renwick. "After all, Georgina, you are attempting the transformation from sow's ear to silk purse. You can't expect it to be easy. Give the waltz another try. Start again, Penelope."

Penelope began anew, and Georgina frowned at Renwick. She was a stubborn young woman, disinclined to giving up easily, but this Sam Botts was making things extremely difficult. A grin appeared on his infuriatingly handsome face. "I'm willing to try again, m'lady, if your ladyship will watch your step. I've a dread of being tramped upon and was reminded o' when our old plowhorse stepped upon my grandfather's foot."

"Old plowhorse? So I remind you of your broken-down horse, do I? Upon my honor, I have never been so insulted by a country oaf who steps as lightly as an elephant in the prince's zoological gardens. I warn you, Sam Botts, you forget who you are and who I am."

To Georgina's dismay Sam Botts did not appear the least bit daunted; he continued to regard her with an insolent grin.

"That is enough," shouted Georgina, turning to her cousin and Victor. "I have had quite enough for one day, Penelope."

"But Georgina, you must teach Sam to dance!"

"Penelope, if you are so eager to have this lout learn to dance, I fear you must teach him yourself. The old plowhorse is returning home. Good day, cousin. Good day, Victor."

Georgina swept out of the room with the haughty demeanor she usually reserved for her forays with certain disapproving society matrons, and Penelope and Victor exchanged startled glances.

"I daresay, Victor," said Penelope, regarding Renwick

suspiciously. "You must teach this rogue some manners."

"I fear," sighed Victor, "that he is incorrigible."

The incorrigible ruffian, who was also the Marquis of Renwick, only shrugged his shoulders.

After leaving Penelope's house, Victor Ballanville's stylish carriage made its way through the busy London streets. Inside, the Marquis of Renwick was staring intently at the passing scene.

"Is it very far to your club?"

"Not far," replied Victor, who was seated beside him. The two cousins were silent for a time, and finally Victor spoke. "Hugh, I think it is time to call off this masquerade. I will not have you upsetting Georgina, and I find the entire business less amusing by the hour. And his grace, the duke, would be furious to find that his only son was pretending to be Sam Botts."

"But I am pretending to be Sam Botts masquerading as myself, so there is little harm in it. And do not worry so about Lady Georgina. That lady is no delicate miss."

"You have an aversion to Georgina that I confess is inexplicable. Everyone loves her."

"Not everyone, Vic. I have disliked her from our first meeting, when I saw her driving like some accursed Amazon, and since then her behavior can hardly be called endearing. But do not worry, I promise I shall try not to upset Lady Georgina."

"I hope so. Oh, it seems we have arrived." The carriage pulled up before a most distinguished example of Georgian architecture, and the cousins alighted from the vehicle and went inside.

The club was deserted except for a middle-aged gentleman, who was sitting alone at a table. The man was staring gloomily into his glass and did not even look up as the two Ballanvilles entered.

"Findlay, old man," said Victor, addressing the gloomy gentleman. "Where the deuce is everyone? Egad, has a plague descended on the place?"

Findlay looked up and stared at Victor with bleary eyes. "Dammit, Ballanville, must you speak so loudly? My head aches like the very devil."

"Sorry, old boy," said Victor in quieter tones. "But where is everyone?"

Findlay put his hands to his head and grimaced. "Oh, that blasted Sir Harvey came in boasting about some new bangup greys he bought. Said they could outrace any horseflesh in London. Of course that ass Bigsby took issue and wagered him to a race. So everyone had to go witness it. Good riddance, I'd say. Hope Harvey and Bigsby break their fool necks."

Victor smiled. "By God, Findlay, you are in a damned disagreeable mood today."

Findlay frowned. "You'd be damned disagreeable, too, if you'd just lost five hundred pounds to old Chartwell."

"The devil, you say!" exclaimed Victor loudly, and when he saw Findlay wince, he continued in a more modulated voice. "To old Chartwell? That is damnable. But buck up, old man, it's only money, after all."

"Only money? Damned insensitive you are, Ballanville. I'm blasted fond of the stuff."

Victor grinned. "Ain't we all? But Findlay, I must introduce you to someone." He turned to Renwick, and that gentleman stepped forward. Findlay looked at the marquis for the first time, and his face lit up in sudden recognition.

"By God, you don't have to tell me who this is. You're the very picture of old Renwick. Or I should say the duke, now."

Renwick smiled. "The duke is my father."

"I knew it. You're just like him. Knew him well, I did, but that was thirty years ago. Haven't seen him since he stole Lady Agnes Fairchild off to that Godforsaken province of his. Don't know that I'll ever forgive him for that."

"My dear Findlay," said Victor in surprise. "You had a *tendre* for my aunt?"

Findlay nodded. "Dammit, Ballanville, half the bucks in London were in love with her. By God, she was a beautiful woman! Dashed clever, too. And how she could make me laugh. Damned sorry I was to hear of her death. But sit down, young Renwick, and tell me about your father." As the marquis and Victor Ballanville sat down, Findlay called for the waiter to bring glasses and another bottle. Renwick then told about his father, and Findlay began to reminisce about when the duke had come to London some thirty-one years before. This amiable conversation had been going on nearly an hour when another gentleman entered the club. The gentleman looked wearily about him, and his gaze fell on the club's only occupants. Normally, the Viscount Milford would have barely acknowledged the presence of the gentlemen sitting at the table. In fact, he usually made it a point to snub Mr. Findlay, since he heartily disliked that gentleman. However, when he observed Renwick at the table, he correctly guessed who he was and leisurely made his way over toward them.

"Ballanville," he said, in a tone that implied he was doing that gentleman a favor by his acknowledgment. The viscount ignored Findlay, who scowled down at his drink.

"Milford," replied Victor coolly, and, noting that the viscount made no move to leave, reluctantly added, "Do sit down."

Milford smiled condescendingly and sat next to the marquis. He turned his gaze to that gentleman and then looked expectantly at Victor.

"Oh, Milford," said Victor, taking the hint, "you haven't met my cousin, the Marquis of Renwick. Lord Renwick, this is Viscount Milford."

"How do," said Milford, shaking Renwick's hand and critically scrutinizing his appearance. He was disappointed to find that the "provincial bumpkin" from the north was a handsome young man who was dressed quite fashionably and seemed not at all unsure of himself. "I heard you were coming to town, Renwick. I believe this is your first visit, is it not?"

"Yes."

"Dear me," replied the viscount, shaking his head. "That is amazing. I can scarcely imagine it. To think you have lived in the far northlands and are only now come to town. But thank God you finally are arrived in civilization."

"I take it you've been in the north, then?" returned the marquis, with a trace of irritation in his voice.

"Most assuredly not," replied Milford disdainfully. "But I imagine it is even drearier than some of those dreadful watering holes that I am forced to endure."

Victor saw Renwick's anger and smiled. "You seem to know something of my cousin, Milford."

"Oh, not really. Lady Georgina Suttondale mentioned that you were coming for a visit." He smiled patronizingly at Renwick. "In fact, I promised the lady I would help introduce you to society."

"Did you?"

"Yes. I know being in London for the first time must be somewhat intimidating for you. After all, when one is not familiar with society—"

Victor burst out laughing. "I can see, Milford, that you don't know my cousin at all. Hugh ain't one to be intimidated, especially by some stodgy old society patronesses."

Findlay smiled. "Just like his papa. He never gave a damn what anyone thought of him. Except Agnes Fairchild."

Milford frowned at Findlay and turned back to Renwick. "My offer still stands, Renwick. I did promise the Lady Georgina, after all."

Renwick smiled. "I am touched by the lady's concern for me, but I haven't required a nursemaid for some time now."

Milford shrugged. "As you wish."

"It appears, Milford," commented Victor nonchalantly, "that you have become rather attentive to my fiancée's cousin of late."

His lordship smiled smugly. "I do enjoy the lady's company." He looked questioningly at Renwick. "You have met the Lady Georgina then?"

"Aye," replied Renwick. "I've met the lady."

Findlay chuckled. "She's a rare one, is Lady Georgina. Damned good-looking female, too. I'll never forget the time she won two hundred pounds from old Sir Benedict. Her papa, the old earl, was always boasting about Georgina, and one day he wagered Benedict that she could even beat him at cards. Sir Benedict refused at first. Said it was ridiculous playing a schoolgirl. By God, she must've been about twelve at the time. But he finally agreed, thinking it would cease Rumbridge's boasting. And damn if the little chit didn't win two hundred pounds from him, easy as you please."

"Really, Findlay," interrupted the viscount, "I'm sure the lady would not appreciate such stories bandied about."

Victor smiled. "What nonsense, Milford. Georgina's quite proud of beating old Sir Benedict. It's Benedict who don't want that story bandied about."

Renwick laughed, and Findlay shook his head. "Damn

shame she's under her brother's guardianship now. Young Rumbridge is a cold fish. Not at all like the old earl."

"I think the lady is lucky to be under her brother's guardianship," said Milford, frowning. "I would not want to say anything against her father, but old Rumbridge had no sense at all in raising the girl. Made her too independent for her own good. After all, there is nothing worse than a headstrong female. But fortunately for the lady, her brother's influence has not been too late, and I daresay all she needs now is a husband who will take a firm rein with her."

"And you think you could be such a husband, Milford?"

"Wives are not so unlike horses, Ballanville, and when one establishes himself as master, there is little problem. A high-spirited filly like Lady Georgina needs but a tight check rein and a firm hand. Do not fear, gentlemen, Lady Milford would be very different from Lady Georgina."

"Indeed," said Victor, "they *will* be two different ladies, for I doubt Lady Georgina would agree to marry you. She is not the sort to meekly join any man's 'stable.'"

"What do you mean by that, Ballanville?"

"I mean, sir, that you are hardly discreet in your affairs. All of London knows how you flaunt your paramours in such an outrageous fashion. If you hope to take Lady Georgina to wife, I suggest you toss aside a few of those ladies of yours."

Milford was suddenly furious. "So you dare to lecture me, Ballanville! I take such talk as highly insulting."

"Oh, I pray you, Milford, do not get so damned upset. I have no desire for you to call me out. I do not intend giving you the satisfaction of killing me in a duel, as I know you would. I am only giving you a word of advice."

Milford rose from his chair. "I don't need your advice, Ballanville. Good day."

Milford left angrily, and Findlay shook his head. "Never could tolerate that fellow."

"Aye," said Renwick, "even Lady Georgina does not deserve him."

"What!" cried Findlay. "Lady Georgina is the kindest, most charming lady."

"So everyone tells me," said Renwick, and he smiled at Findlay's shocked expression.

6

As Smallbone went about his duties, he reflected on the sorry business of the last few days. It was bad enough that his employer's fiancée had mistaken the Marquis of Renwick for a servant. Not that Smallbone blamed Miss Amesbury and the Lady Georgina, since the marquis had presented such a shabby appearance. But for Mr. Ballanville and Lord Renwick to continue the deception, and even go so far as involve him in it, was quite infamous! Of course it was not his place to judge his betters, but Smallbone could not help but disapprove of the whole situation. As he mulled over these unpleasant thoughts, Smallbone heard a knock on the door. He quickly went to answer it, and opened the door to a tall, imposing gentleman who quickly doffed his hat and made a theatrical bow.

"Mr. Ritchie to see Mr. Ballanville."

"Of course, sir," said Smallbone, who was very well aware of the identity of this exalted personage. "Come in, please." The servant ushered him into the small sitting room and then dutifully hurried off to inform his master. Kenneth Ritchie sat down on the sofa and gazed about the room as if it were a new stage set. Soon Victor Ballanville and Renwick entered the room, and Ritchie stood up and smiled.

"Ritchie," said Victor, with a broad smile, "it is good of you to come. We do appreciate your helping us, you know."

"Thank you, Mr. Ballanville." He paused and nodded at Renwick. "Shall we begin then . . . my lord?"

"Oh, do call me Renwick," said the young man nonchalantly as he dropped into a chair. Ritchie grinned.

"Your lordship is most kind."

Renwick lounged back in his chair and smiled. "Well, Ritchie, tell me then, how do I act a lord?"

Ritchie looked at Victor Ballanville. "Oh, don't mind me," said Victor, with a bemused expression. "I am quite interested in knowing myself."

Ritchie smiled and turned back to Renwick. "All right, then. First things first, my boy. If you're to act a lord, the heir to a dukedom, mind you, you must have the proper air about you. That air of condescension that says 'I am better than the whole bloody lot of you!'" To demonstrate, Ritchie tilted his chin up and eyed Renwick with such a haughty expression that the young marquis burst into laughter.

"You must view the world from your lofty heights with a great deal of disdain and boredom." Ritchie stood up and walked over to the mantel. He leaned back against it and absently twirled his quizzing glass, looking wearily about the room. "Few things, you see, are worthy of your attention."

He paused, and Renwick grinned. "Do go on, sir."

"Yes," agreed Victor, "I daresay this is quite enlightening for his lordship here."

Renwick nodded and continued. "Your lordship, as a proper gentleman, does of course have some interests in life. These are, namely, horses, any kind of sport a'tall, drinking, and wenching."

"But not necessarily in that order," murmured Victor.

Renwick laughed. "Sounds a damned hard life. But do tell me more, Ritchie." The actor smiled, pleased as always by such an attentive audience, and proceeded to inform the marquis further about proper lordly behavior.

A couple hours had passed when Ritchie's session with Renwick was interrupted by the appearance of Smallbone. That worthy servant was amazed to open the door and find the Marquis of Renwick repeating rhymes of a most ridiculous nature. The actor Kenneth Ritchie appeared to be listening attentively, and when Renwick finished, he beamed.

"Good, good, my boy. Damned remarkable how quick you are!"

"Thank you," replied Renwick, grinning immodestly, and Victor Ballanville almost burst out laughing. He looked over at the door and, at the sight of Smallbone's astonished expression, did burst out laughing.

"Smallbone?" he finally said with some semblance of dignity.

The servant had also regained his composure, and replied in an expressionless voice, "Miss Amesbury and the Lady Georgina to see you, sir."

"Oh, do send them in."

Smallbone nodded perfunctorily and left, only to return a moment later to announce the ladies. Penelope hurried into the room and, after a quick greeting to Victor, advanced on Ritchie.

"So tell us, sir, how is Sam progressing? Georgie and I are so very curious."

However, the Lady Georgina did not at all appear curious. She came into the room, nodded to Victor and Ritchie, and sat down. Only then did the lady cast a quick, indifferent glance at Renwick. He did not smile at her as he met her glance, but his eyes held a look of amusement.

Kenneth Ritchie smiled broadly at Penelope and Georgina. "I should think, dear ladies, that you will win your wager easily."

"Do you think so?" asked Penelope.

"Yes. Sam here is a remarkable fellow. Best student I've ever had. Picks up on things quick as anything."

"Oh that's wonderful news!" cried Penelope. "But then I knew Sam was a clever fellow."

"Dashed clever," agreed Ritchie. "Of course, he needs a bit more work on his speech, but I tell you, ladies, I think he could fool anyone." He turned to the marquis. "I must say I've never seen such a natural talent for acting, except of course," he added with a smile, "in myself. Have you ever considered the stage, my boy?"

"No," replied Renwick. "I can't say I have."

Victor grinned. "I should think the stage would suit you much better than being a footman, Sam."

Penelope nodded enthusiastically. "I daresay Sam could become famous."

"Infamous, more likely," murmured Georgina.

"What, coz?" asked Penelope, turning to her.

"Oh, nothing," said Georgina.

At that moment Smallbone entered the room. "Your carriage is here, Mr. Ritchie."

"Oh yes, blast," said Kenneth Ritchie. "I am afraid I must be going now. I have a rehearsal with Mrs. Terrell."

"You're a fortunate man," said Renwick.

Ritchie smiled. "You could be, too, Sam. Just say the word and I will arrange things. There is a small part that I could get you . . ."

"A *small* part?" inquired the marquis, with eyebrows raised.

Ritchie laughed. "Damned if I shan't regret encouraging you, my boy." He nodded to him, said farewell to Victor and the ladies, and made his exit.

"Well!" said Penelope. "You certainly made an impression on Kenneth Ritchie, Sam. What did you learn?"

"Well, miss, Mr. Ritchie told me all about how a lord should behave."

Or misbehave, thought Victor, smiling.

"I hope you do as Mr. Ritchie tells you," said Georgina, finally addressing Renwick. He nodded at her with mock solemnity. "I'll do my best, m'lady."

Georgina thought she detected sarcasm in his voice, but she decided it best to ignore it. "Yes; well, then, Penelope, I suppose we can go."

"Go? But we just got here, Georgie."

"Yes, do stay, Georgina," said Victor. He looked at his cousin and smiled. "I was just going to give Sam another lesson."

"Oh?"

"Yes. I thought I'd better tell him all about his family. Or rather my cousin Renwick's family. I mean, one should know about that sort of thing to be at all convincing."

Penelope smiled. "Oh, dear, yes. Sam must know all about the Ballanvilles, or our masquerade could be quite disastrous." She turned to her cousin. "Come, let's stay a little while, Georgie. Victor tells the most amusing stories about the old duke."

Victor Ballanville and his cousin exchanged glances as Georgina shrugged. "Very well." She sat down, and they all looked at Victor.

"All right, I shall tell you of the Ballanvilles." He turned to Renwick. "Now you must try to memorize this carefully, Sam. You mustn't trip up, you know."

Renwick smiled. "I swear that before this is over I'll know the Ballanvilles better than you, sir."

Victor nodded. "Very good, Sam. Now first there is your father, Horace Ballanville, the twelfth Duke of Welham."

"Excuse me, Mr. Ballanville," interrupted Renwick. "Duke of what?"

"Welham . . . *well um*," he pronounced slowly.

"Welham," repeated Renwick. "I do have it now."

"Capital. Anyway, the duke, my Uncle Horace, is a right enough old fellow, but damned tight with his blunt—of which I might say he has plenty."

"Tough old skinflint, eh?" remarked Renwick.

"Precisely," smiled Victor.

"And he never comes to London?" asked Georgina curiously.

"No. Oh, he visited here as a young man, of course. That's when he met my Aunt Agnes. Carried her off, he did, to that medieval castle of his."

"Oh, dear," said Georgina, "it sounds like the plot in some dreadful novel."

Victor laughed. "I suppose it does. But in any case my aunt doted on the duke and did not seem to mind being away from civilization. Of course, mama prevailed on her to visit London now and again, but after she started having her family, we would go up to Welham to visit. God, I loved going there as a boy. My cousin Hugh and I had such devilish fun."

Georgina smiled at the nostalgic look on Victor's face. "You haven't been there for some time, have you, Vic?"

He shook his head regretfully. "No, it's been over two years. I haven't been there since my aunt's death." He looked apologetically at Renwick, knowing what unhappy memories he had stirred. "But I should tell you about the rest of the family. There is, of course, my cousin Hugh. That is you, of course. He is the duke's only son, and a good fellow—the best, in fact, and like a brother to me. Of course, he is shockingly provincial." He looked at Renwick and grinned.

"My dear, how could he not be?" asked Penelope. She

sighed. "Imagine living one's whole life in some wilderness!"

"Really, coz," said Georgina, "you make it sound like he is living in America amidst savages. It is England, after all."

"And a prettier part of England you'll never see, m'lady," said Renwick. "I'm from up north myself," he added quickly.

"Yes, Victor said you were from the north," said Georgina in a surprised tone. "But I have got the impression you were anxious to get away from there and come to London."

Renwick shrugged. "London be an exciting place, m'lady, especially for a country fellow like myself. But my home be elsewhere."

"*Is* elsewhere, Sam, *is*," said Victor in mock exasperation. "Don't forget your speech. And I must say your affection for your home is quite touching. You sound very much like old Hugh."

Renwick smiled at his cousin and turned back to Georgina. "Has your ladyship never been up north?"

Georgina smiled. "When I was a girl, papa went fishing near Brackendale and took me along. It was beautiful. Such a wild, romantic place. I have often wished to go back."

"Brackendale," said the marquis in surprise, "why that's—"

"Very close to Welham," supplied Victor quickly.

"Well, coz," said Penelope, "once Vic and I are married we must visit the Ballanvilles and take you with us. Who knows, it might prove diverting. But do tell us more about your cousin, Victor. Do you think he'll be angry when he finds out about Sam taking his place?"

"Hmmm . . ." said Victor thoughtfully. "Hugh does have a devilish quick temper, but I suspect he'll think it a great joke. Hugh does love a good laugh."

"He does not at all sound like the duke," said Georgina. "I mean, the duke sounds rather grim."

Victor laughed. "Oh, the duke is a lovable enough old curmudgeon. Just doesn't like to spend his blunt, is all."

Renwick shook his head. "Ain't natural, but the nobs do have their quirks."

Georgina frowned at him, and he grinned. Renwick then turned to Victor.

"And are there other Ballanvilles?"

"Oh, yes; let me see. There's Hugh's four sisters, Mary, Jane, Lucy, and Lizzie. Mary is the oldest. She's three years older than you—or Renwick, that is. That would make her nine and twenty. She's married to a Scottish gentleman, Sir Alex MacKenzie. They have four children, or is it five? Oh, of course, you wouldn't know, would you? I believe it is four. And then Jane is two years younger than I. I am the same age as Renwick, I might add. That makes Jane four and twenty. She's married to Lord Howison, who is a good chap, and they have a little daughter, I think. Lucy and Lizzie are twins. Egad, they're sixteen now."

"And do you expect me to learn all of them, Mr. Ballanville?" said Renwick.

"Certainly, my good man. And in addition there are aunts and uncles and a good many cousins."

"Good lord," muttered Renwick, trying not to smile. "How's this Renwick ever keep them all straight?"

"Oh, he's a clever fellow, Cousin Hugh," said Victor, grinning. "And he's very serious about most things. He's dashed popular among his father's tenants, and he's always making some improvements on the estate. A man of the soil, don't you know. A wizard about agricultural science."

"Oh, how dreary he sounds, Victor," said Penelope. "But you really must insist he come to London. He is a gentleman of rank and must learn of life in town. Wouldn't you agree, coz?"

Georgina nodded. "Most assuredly. You must help your cousin escape from his dull life of country farmer. But I daresay he had better not appear in the next couple of weeks. We can't have two Renwicks about town."

"I can assure you, Georgina, that will not happen," said Victor. "I would bet on it." Victor Ballanville took on such an amused expression as he said these words that Georgina regarded him curiously.

7

LORD RENWICK DID NOT SEE LADY GEORGINA Suttondale again for three days, and, as he told Victor, the lady's absence made his stay in London much more pleasant. Victor was shocked at the remark, but admitted that Lady Georgina did seem less than enamored of his cousin.

They did call upon Miss Penelope Amesbury each afternoon, but Lady Georgina was not there. As Penelope explained, she had been entrapped by her brother Rumbridge and forced to spend a few days visiting her sister-in-law's relatives, including the formidable Lady Quarles, patroness of Almack's.

Although Renwick was relieved to find Georgina absent each time they called upon Miss Amesbury, he was also a trifle disappointed. He disliked the proud young lady with the brown eyes. That he knew well enough; but he also had a perverse joy in irritating her. He enjoyed the way her eyes flashed at him and the way her lovely mouth set into a disapproving frown at his words. He spent much time during those days thinking about the Lady Georgina, but he would sooner have been racked than admit this to his cousin.

Fortunately, there were so many diversions that Renwick had little time for reflection. Victor was intent upon showing him London, and they were active from noon, when they got up, until the early predawn hours, when they returned home. The day was filled with continuous activity. They attended a horse race, three bouts of fisticuffs, and a cock fight, which Renwick, being an animal lover and soft-hearted despite his rather stern demeanor, did not enjoy.

At Penelope's house Renwick met the painter Falconrest and again met Sir Swithin Baxter and the disagreeable Mrs. Grove, who usually tried to stay out of Penelope's way. He was not sure what to think of Penelope. She was scatterbrained and silly; and she said some very shocking things to Sir Swithin Baxter, who replied with even more shocking comments. Yet, shocking as they were, nothing the elderly gentleman said caused a blush to appear on Penelope's fair cheeks. Renwick found it difficult to dislike his cousin's beloved Penelope, but he decided she and her wayward friend Georgina were not the type of ladies he preferred.

He did, however, meet a young lady more to his taste when walking with Victor. Lady Dunstan Carlyle, accompanied by her daughter the honorable Miss Emily Carlyle, came upon them while the two cousins were strolling through the park on the way to call upon Victor's friend Richard Averton. Lady Dunstan was one of Victor's Marshfield cousins and had married the second son of the Duke of Moncrieffe. Fortunately for Lady Dunstan, her husband, though a second son, was exceedingly shrewd and had taken his meager inheritance and turned it into a comfortable fortune.

"Victor," said Lady Dunstan, regarding him fondly.

"Cousin Kate and Cousin Emily."

Miss Emily Carlyle smiled demurely at Victor. She was a tiny, delicate creature with reddish brown hair, a creamy complexion, and a wide-eyed innocence that Renwick found very appealing.

"Ladies, I should like to present my cousin Hugh, Marquis of Renwick. Hugh, this is my cousin Lady Dunstan Carlyle, and her daughter, Miss Emily Carlyle."

Renwick took first Lady Dunstan's hand, and then Miss Emily's. He was amazed at the daintiness of her hand, which was dwarfed by his own.

"My cousin is visiting London for the first time," explained Victor.

"I do hope you are enjoying yourself," said Lady Dunstan.

"Indeed I am, ma'am," said Renwick, glancing sidelong at Miss Emily, who regarded him shyly for a moment and then cast her blue eyes downward with what Renwick considered to be charming modesty.

"I hope you gentlemen will excuse us," said Lady Dunstan, but we have an engagement and must be getting along. But, Victor, I insist that you and Lord Renwick call upon us very soon. I know you gentlemen are always busy, but I shall not forgive you if you do not call."

"I shall indeed, dear Kate," said Victor, and the ladies continued on their way. Renwick watched them go with what seemed to Victor more than passing interest.

"What is this, Cousin Hugh? Don't tell me you have been charmed by my little cousin. By God, Hugh, she is only a child—and a very spoiled child, I might add."

"I thought her a very well-mannered young lady."

"She is a little mouse."

Better a mouse, thought Renwick, than a she-cat like Lady Georgina. "She is rather young looking," remarked Renwick.

"Seventeen. This is her first season, and already she has dozens of suitors. I daresay I doubt my little cousin will remain unmarried very long."

"Hmmm . . ." Renwick looked thoughtful.

"Oh, Hugh! You're not thinking that you might be another of her suitors? My dear cousin, I know you are under orders from the duke to think about matrimony, but I assure you my cousin Emily is not the girl for you. No, you and I are too much alike. You must find a woman more like my Penelope. Like Georgina, for instance."

"Are you mad, Victor?"

Victor laughed at his cousin's expression. "Oh, let us talk no more of your marital plans. Come, I want you to meet Richard."

Renwick continued on, thinking of Miss Emily Carlyle and the great contrast between this quiet little lady and the wild Lady Georgina.

The "wild" Lady Georgina had been having a very miserable three days traveling about town, visiting a number of people she would gladly never have seen again. Her sister-in-law's relations were a very stodgy lot. In general they did not approve of her, nor did they approve of her friends.

It had been extremely difficult to keep from making

rude replies when Amelia's sister commented about the outrageous behavior of "certain young ladies." Georgina knew very well that she was included in this unfortunate group, and it was only through a monumental exercise of self-control that she refrained from giving the Lady Quarles a well-deserved set-down.

However, Georgina's self-control gave Amelia little cause to criticize her, and Rumbridge was rather pleased about her behavior. After three days of making calls, Amelia had thought a quiet day at home was in order. Therefore, she took up her needlework and joined Georgina, who was sitting in the drawing room reading a book.

"Really, Georgina, you will ruin your eyes reading so much," remarked the countess, looking disapprovingly at her sister-in-law and then sitting down beside her.

Georgina looked up from her book. "Oh, don't worry, Amelia, if my eyes go bad I'll just get myself a pair of spectacles."

"Spectacles!" cried the countess in dismay, and Georgina laughed.

Lady Rumbridge shook her head and began to work on her embroidery. "It is not a joking matter, Georgina," she said coolly. "Men do not approve of bookish ladies. You should spend your time developing more suitable accomplishments."

"What nonsense," scoffed Georgina, who had grown quite weary of being diplomatic.

At that moment her brother walked in and turned his weak smile upon them. "What's nonsense, Georgina?"

"Oh, Amelia thinks I should spend more time developing more 'suitable' accomplishments."

The earl nodded. "And Amelia's right."

His wife smiled at him and then looked frostily at Georgina. "Yes, you could devote more practice to your stitchery, for example."

Georgina laughed. "I daresay I could, but I do not care for stitchery. It is difficult to like something you are not at all good at."

Her sister-in-law frowned. "That is only because you never got enough practice as a girl. I think it's abominable that your father neglected your proper education."

"He did not!" cried Georgina indignantly. "I had an admirable education with Liddy."

The earl shook his head. "The eccentric Miss Liddcott? Not my idea of a governess. If I recall she had some very singular ideas about things. She did not believe in discipline."

The countess frowned. "It is important for a young girl to have discipline."

He nodded solemnly. "Of course it is, Amelia. But my father wasn't one for discipline where Georgina was concerned."

The countess shook her head and regarded her sister-in-law sadly. Georgina smiled. "Oh, don't look so tragic, Amelia. I may not be proficient at stitchery and watercolor painting, but I am quite good at driving a four-in-hand." As Georgina had wickedly anticipated, her comment brought another cry of dismay from the countess.

"I knew your behavior these past three days was only an act, Georgina. It seems you are again showing your true colors."

"Georgina," began her brother sternly; but he was interrupted by the appearance of Tabb, who announced that Miss Amesbury and Mrs. Grove were waiting.

"Oh, send her in, Tabb," said the earl. He was surprised, since Penelope Amesbury made very infrequent visits to the Rumbridge house. The earl frowned, but greeted his cousin civilly when she entered the room. In turn she smiled at him.

"Rummy!" she said, using the pet name that she knew he despised. "How good to see you." She then greeted the countess, who gave her a forced smile.

"Penelope, Mrs. Grove, won't you sit down?"

"Oh, thank you, Amelia, but we don't have time. We just came to fetch Georgina." She looked over to where Georgina sat, her book still propped on her lap, and turned to Rumbridge. "I do hope you will not object to Georgina's accompanying us. I have not seen her at all for three days, and we must do some shopping. My wedding grows nearer, you see."

Lady Rumbridge, who was quickly tiring of Georgina's company, was not averse to her leaving, despite her hearty disapproval of Penelope Amesbury.

"I do think we could spare Georgina, could we not, Rumbridge?"

Lord Rumbridge looked at his wife in some surprise, but nodded.

"How good of you, Robert," said Georgina. "I shall be back early." She hurriedly went to get her bonnet and pelisse; but as they were leaving, the earl asked warily, "Are you driving your phaeton, Penelope?"

She looked at him and shook her head. "Oh, don't worry, old cousin. I'm not driving. In fact I have a very respectable driver, so you can feel quite at ease."

The Earl of Rumbridge nodded, and the two cousins and Mrs. Grove left the house. As Tabb opened the door, Georgina spied her cousin's high-perch phaeton in front of the house.

"And where's your respectable driver, coz?"

Penelope laughed. "Right here. You can drive, Georgie."

Georgina laughed and shook her head. "You are dreadful. And Rumbridge may be watching. What's this all about?"

"Oh, I told Vic we'd meet him and Sam in the park and thought it would be easier to say we were going shopping. Although I daresay Amelia would've been quite pleased to hear you were going to spend the afternoon with the Marquis of Renwick."

Georgina frowned. "I do not intend to spend an afternoon with Sam Botts."

Penelope laughed. "Really, coz, don't be ridiculous. Sam is not such a bad fellow. I like him, in fact. And I do think he would be rather good on the stage, don't you?"

Georgina shrugged, but didn't reply. As they got into the phaeton, Georgina took the reins, and soon they were on their way. Several heads turned toward them as they rode down the streets, and Georgina shook her head.

"Rumbridge isn't going to like this. He doesn't approve of my driving."

Penelope smiled. "Well, I daresay he approves of your driving more than he approves of mine." She glanced back at Mrs. Grove, who sat looking very stern. "And I daresay Mrs. Grove is none too happy about this," whispered Penelope. "She would prefer being at home."

Georgina smiled. "I think you're right there, coz. Poor Mrs. Grove." Poor Mrs. Grove continued to stare grimly at the passing scenery.

They soon arrived at the park, and Penelope spied Victor Ballanville and Sam Botts. Victor waved, and he and Renwick walked toward the phaeton. Georgina expertly pulled the vehicle over, and she looked down to find Renwick staring up at her.

"Afternoon, m'lady," he said, slipping easily into his Sam Botts role. She gave him a formal greeting and then hesitated. Victor was helping Penelope down, so she had little choice but to let Renwick assist her from the phaeton. He seemed none too pleased with the task, reluctantly offering her his hand.

"Thank you so very much," she said sarcastically after he had helped her down. "I see how painful it was for you to help me."

"I suppose it is my job," he said, and then turned to assist Mrs. Grove from the vehicle.

Georgina was startled by his rudeness, but decided she would simply ignore him. He is but a footman, she told herself, not for the first time, and then turned to Victor.

"And so, dear Victor, have you been enjoying yourself these three days since I last saw you?"

"Indeed, yes, Georgina. I have been working diligently at Sam's lessons. He is the perfect gentleman now."

"Is he?" remarked Georgina, eyeing him coldly.

"We have been to my club and to the races, and he has met Averton and Lord Durham and all manner of people, and there is no one who is not convinced that he is indeed my cousin."

"You see, Georgina, it was a marvelous idea. And poor Swithin loses his three hundred pounds! But he can well afford it. But come, let us go for a ride. The day is lovely and perfect for driving. Come along, Georgie, you shall drive us all about town."

"She'll drive?" cried Renwick in his exaggerated north country accent. "I'll not be riding in any vehicle she'll be driving! Mr. Ballanville, my life means too much to me."

"Good," snapped Georgina. "Then you shall walk!"

"Oh dear," said Victor, somewhat alarmed, "let us not argue. Now Sam, don't be unreasonable. Georgina is a fine driver, and she'll promise to keep them well under control, won't you, Georgina?"

"I don't think Mr. Botts should be forced to risk his life by riding with me."

"Right you are," said Renwick. "I think it's a man's place to drive."

"And no one cares for your opinion," said Georgina. There was a dangerous gleam in her eye.

"Oh, don't be silly," said Penelope, stepping in as peacemaker. "Of course you'll drive, Georgina. Victor and I and Mrs. Grove will ride back here, and you will drive with Sam up beside you."

"I think not," said Georgina.

"And I think not, too. I'll ride in back."

Mrs. Grove regarded them all scornfully and, without a word, climbed into the back seat of the phaeton. Penelope laughed. "You see, Mrs. Grove is quite perturbed by all of this. Come, Vic." Penelope climbed into the carriage, assisted by Victor, who followed close behind.

The only course now open to Renwick was to hand Georgina up into the driver's seat and climb up beside her. Georgina took the reins and, with a contemptuous look at Renwick, took up the whip and snapped it smartly, causing the horses to take off so abruptly that Renwick was nearly thrown from his seat.

"Good God," he muttered, but Georgina ignored him and guided the horse down the street at a pace Renwick thought far too fast for town. She slowed them after a time, and Renwick breathed easier; before long he grudgingly realized that she did have considerable skill with the ribbons. He noted that one of the lead horses had a tendency to pull to the right, but Georgina soon corrected that and kept the spirited animal well under control.

"Perhaps you're not so unskilled as I thought," said Renwick aloud.

She looked at him in some surprise. "You amaze me! Don't tell me you've lost your fear of death at my hands?"

"I'm still a bit nervous being driven by a female," he replied, and Georgina frowned and concentrated on the horses.

They traveled several miles and were soon in a section of town crowded with vehicles of every description. Georgina slowed her horses to a walk in the heavy traffic.

"Pleasant place you've brought us to, m'lady," said Renwick. "Good you know your way around so well."

"I'll thank you to keep quiet!" she said angrily. "It is difficult enough without your complaints!"

Georgina turned her horses from the main street into a narrow lane and here, at the sight of a car blocking the way, pulled her horses up short. The dilapidated old cart was piled high with barrels, and harnessed to it was a solitary little horse.

A burly, unkempt man was standing in front, tugging at the animal's head. "Dammit, you crow bait. Move, or I'll feed you to the dogs!"

The little horse strained for a moment and then stopped, and the man angrily took up an evil-looking stick and hit the horse hard across its flanks.

"Brute!" cried Georgina, horrified. She thrust the reins into Renwick's hands and jumped down from the phaeton with a most unladylike leap, her whip in her hand.

"Brute!" she cried again, and the burly man looked up in surprise to see a well-dressed and very angry young lady approaching. "How dare you treat a helpless creature in such a fashion. I should take my whip to you!"

The man glared at her. "'Tis no business of yours, miss! Stand back and I'll get this nag moving."

"You've overloaded her. You can't expect her to pull such a load. You'll kill her!"

"She's my horse, miss, and I'll kill her if I damned well please!" He spat contemptuously on the ground. "I don't need fine ladies like you telling me how to treat my own horse. Now you get out of my way or I'll take my stick to you first!"

Georgina looked horrified, and the vile-looking man took a step toward her, brandishing his stick in a threatening manner.

"I think not," said a masculine voice, and two powerful hands reached out and grasped the man by the collar. He was so surprised he dropped the stick he had been using to beat his poor horse.

"Now that isn't any way to talk to the lady," said the Marquis of Renwick angrily. He looked quite formidable, and the man quailed.

"I wasn't meaning no offense, sir," he said.

Renwick smiled scornfully and released him. He looked from the man to his horse. It was indeed a sorry-looking creature. The roan mare was exhausted, and she had numerous scars on her back that bore witness to her brutal treatment. Renwick doubted the creature would survive much longer under such a master. He looked down at the ground and picked up the stick.

"Damned if I shouldn't take this to your hide."

"I ain't done nothing," protested the man. "The blasted horse wouldn't obey me."

Georgina walked over and patted the horse on the head. It regarded her with sad brown eyes. "Poor thing," she said. She turned back to the man. "You should be put in prison," she declared angrily.

"I ain't done nothing," he said again. "This horse be my property. I can't be blocking the street, now can I? How's your fine carriage to get through?"

There was genuine hatred in the man's eyes, and Georgina was glad of Renwick's presence.

"If you would treat her right, you should have far better use of her. And she's too small for such a load." Georgina rubbed the horse's head affectionately. "Come on, little one," she said, taking the reins. "Come a few more steps. Come on."

The little mare strained one more time, and the cart slowly moved. "A bit more," urged Georgina, and the horse struggled a few more yards until the way was clear.

"Whoa, then," said Georgina, regarding the burly man with disgust. "You see, she'll try if she's not beaten, but she can go no farther under such a load! Unhitch her!"

"What?" The burly man was bewildered. "'Tis my horse! My property!"

"I shall buy her from you!"

"You will not!" protested the burly man.

"Won't she?" Renwick looked at the burly man, a dangerous expression on his face.

"I'll not be cheated!"

"Be quiet," said Renwick. "You'll be compensated. Unhitch the horse!"

The man muttered an oath, but unhitched the poor animal, and Georgina pulled two gold coins from her reticule. After the horse was unhitched, she tossed them at the man.

"This ain't hardly enough," he cried, feigning indignation; he was really quite happy with the sum. "You're stealing my horse, you are."

"Shut up, man," said Renwick, with a menacing gesture. He led the mare back to the phaeton and, to Victor's and Penelope's surprise, tied her to the back of the carriage. He then helped Georgina up into the seat and climbed up himself. Georgina took the reins again, and they were off. As they passed the burly man and his cart, he shouted at them, but Georgina paid no attention.

Penelope and Victor had watched the entire scene with great interest.

"By God," shouted Victor. "That was marvelous, coming to the old girl's rescue." He looked back at the horse, which, now relieved of her burden, was doing quite well. "Looks like you've got a real bargain there, Georgina. A sorrier hack I've never seen."

"She only needs some care," said Georgina. "And she shall get it in Penelope's stables."

"My stables?" cried Penelope.

Georgina laughed and looked over at Renwick. "I could not possibly take her home to Rumbridge's house."

They continued on for a while, and Georgina glanced over at Renwick, who was looking at her with a curious expression. "Don't stare at me so, Sam Botts!"

He smiled at her. "You do have a temper, don't you, Lady Georgina?"

"I, a temper? I daresay, Sam Botts, it is your temper that is much more fearsome." She paused. "I do thank you, Sam."

He was taken aback by her expression and could barely manage to reply. " 'Twas nothing at all." This sudden lack of enmity seemed to embarrass them both, and they said nothing more. The phaeton continued down the street, and many people stopped to watch the elegant vehicle, its smart, high-stepping chestnuts followed by a pathetic little roan mare tied behind.

8

"I SAY, HUGH," SAID VICTOR BALLANVILLE when he and his cousin had returned home. "Dashed funny about Georgina and that miserable nag. Georgina has such a soft heart."

"Does she?" said Renwick. "I must admit it surprises me to hear it."

Victor looked over at his cousin, who had just seated himself on the sofa. "What is the matter with you, Hugh? You are acting strangely."

"Oh, I don't know. Perhaps you are right. Perhaps this game is being taken too far. I'm growing tired of it."

"Perhaps you are growing tired of having the Lady Georgina think of you as only a footman."

"You are speaking nonsense, Victor."

"Am I? I noticed the way you looked at her. I should have horsewhipped Sam Botts for such a look."

"You are mad, Victor! She may be an attractive lady, but she is the wildest and most unreasonable female I have ever met. And I do not approve of ladies jumping down from phaetons and accosting bullies in the street. Now please, Victor, I do not want to say any more about it."

"Very well, cousin," said Victor, with a knowing smile. "Come let's be off to the club. And then tonight we'll go to the theatre, just the two of us. God, we'll have fun. You'll forget all about Georgina and her sorry nag and Sam Botts for a bit. You'll see."

"Why do you think I'm thinking of her at all?" came Renwick lamely. "No, don't say another word. I am ready to be off and enjoy all London has to offer."

Victor grinned. "Then come along, cousin. The town is waiting for us."

Lord Renwick tried not to think about Lady Georgina, but found to his great irritation that this was not possible. Try as he would, he could not keep from picturing that lovely face of hers, with its slightly upturned nose and the dark eyes fringed with long, dark lashes.

Since his lordship found reflecting upon Lady Georgina most irritating, he decided to forget as best he could by consuming unusually large quantities of spirits at Victor's club. Victor was most obliging in this regard, insisting his cousin's glass be filled time and again, until Renwick forgot completely about Georgina and began to enjoy himself immensely.

By the time they arrived at the theatre, Lord Renwick was in a very jolly, though rather inebriated, condition; he therefore viewed the play with great enthusiasm, although little understanding. He recognized Kenneth Ritchie and roared his approval at that gentleman's performance. His lordship's excessive exuberance was not much noted, however, since most of the theatregoers were very vocal in their appreciation of Mr. Ritchie's thespian talents.

Mrs. Terrell, too, gained Lord Renwick's approval, and he repeatedly pronounced her a "dashed fine actress" and "lovely as a goddess." At the conclusion of the performance Renwick amazed Victor by insisting upon visiting the actors backstage. They made their way to Mr. Ritchie's dressing room, and, upon announcing in an imperious voice that he was the Marquis of Renwick, Hugh Ballanville was admitted, with his cousin in tow, by a stagehand.

"God, you were grand, Ritchie," said Renwick, sitting down heavily upon a chair and casting his eyes about the dressing room. It was ornately and yet tastefully furnished and might have been a sitting room for a prince.

"Thank you, Lord Renwick," said Ritchie, eyeing the marquis curiously as he began to remove his costume. "Richard III is not one of my best, I fear."

"Nonsense," said Victor. "It was marvelous."

"Yes, indeed," agreed Renwick.

"I doubt my performance was anyway near as convincing as yours, Renwick."

"Mine?"

Ritchie nodded. "You're very much the noble lord tonight. You look the part, and have been drinking the part, too, I see."

Renwick laughed. "Damn you, I've had a bit, I do admit, but you'll never see the day Hugh Ballanville is too drunk to know what he's doing."

"My, my," said Ritchie, sitting down to remove his makeup. "Even think you're Lord Renwick now, do you? That's very good. Oh, you'd make a fine actor, my boy. I've a place in the troupe if you want it."

"Hear that, Vic—or I should say Mr. Ballanville, shouldn't I?" said Renwick. "I'll be an actor! Sounds like a dashed fine idea to me."

Victor began to look uneasy. "Now, Sam, old fellow, noble lords do not become actors."

"But actors become noble lords, do they not? Why, Ritchie here became a king tonight. It's only fair to have it the other way around. I shall join the troupe and become an actor!"

"Now, Renwick," said Victor, quite alarmed at his cousin's uncharacteristic behavior. When they were boys, it had been Hugh who had been the sobering influence, but now Renwick was acting most odd.

"You are here!" cried a feminine voice, and they looked up to see Fanny Terrell enter, still attired as Lady Anne.

"Ah, dear lady," cried Renwick, leaping to his feet. "You were magnificent!" He grinned at her, and then looked from her heavily painted face to her tightly laced and extremely low-cut bodice. Mrs. Terrell did not seem to mind his bold scrutiny.

"How kind of you to say such things. Oh, how splendid you look, Lord Renwick. You see? It doesn't seem odd at all to call you that. You are very much the proper lord."

"Not so very proper," said Renwick, grasping Mrs. Terrell's hand and kissing it fervently.

"Oh, God," said Victor, glancing at Kenneth Ritchie.

Ritchie shook his head. "In only one lesson he is acting exactly like a noble lord. I should take lessons from him, it appears."

"Dear Mrs. Terrell, won't you join Victor and me for supper?"

"I did have an engagement," began Mrs. Terrell, but a look into Renwick's handsome face and his mischievous blue eyes made her stop. "'Tis nothing important, a bloody French count is all. You wait right there, my dear. I'll be back soon." Mrs. Terrell quickly left, and Renwick sat back down in his chair.

"Can't see Fanny taking up with you, old boy," said Ritchie, taking off the last of his makeup. "After all, beneath that lordly appearance is still Sam Botts."

"Is it, now?" Renwick grinned. "Well, old Sam ain't a bad one either. Oh, Vic, I didn't ask her to bring a friend for you."

"Good lord, I am going home and you are coming with me."

"I am not! You said I'm to have fun, and have fun I will!"

"Egad," muttered Victor, now quite distressed.

"Here I am!" The three men looked up in amazement to see Fanny Terrell, transformed. Dressed in a very daring and revealing gown of green silk that set off her bright-red hair, and covered with gaudy jewels, Mrs. Terrell was ready.

"So soon!" cried Renwick.

Mrs. Terrell winked at him. "I'm a quick one if I've a reason, and you, my handsome friend, are as good a reason as I've had in quite some time."

"Excuse me, gentlemen," said Renwick. "I'll see you later." He bowed to them and grinned, and was gone, leaving his cousin Victor staring after him with a stricken look on his face.

Lord Renwick opened his eyes and moaned. He had a tremendous headache, and he could not remember feeling more miserable. He was lying on his back in bed, and, looking up, he was suddenly astonished at the ceiling. It was covered with painted figures, little cupids with bows and quivers of arrows. "Good God, where am I?" muttered his lordship. He moaned again and, turning to his side, caught sight of a mass of red curls.

"Oh, lord." The marquis pressed his throbbing head with his hand and stared over at the inert form of Fanny Terrell. Mrs. Terrell stirred in her sleep, turning over and thrusting the bedclothes back to reveal an expanse of soft white flesh.

"Oh, lord," repeated Renwick, sitting up in bed and discovering that he was stark naked beneath the rumpled bedclothes. "What in the name of God has happened?" Of course, another look at Fanny Terrell made the nature of the previous night's events appear rather obvious. The throbbing in Renwick's head grew worse as he tried to remember.

With some difficulty he remembered supper and drinking quite a bit of a very delightful wine. And then he had been in a carriage with Fanny, and then they were at her house. "Oh, yes," said Renwick. He did remember the rest. Indeed, Fanny Terrell was not a woman one might forget easily. "Oh, God," he said again.

"Sam?" Fanny opened her eyes and regarded him with a sleepy smile. "Oh Sam, good morning—or is it afternoon? I don't care. Oh Sam," she said again, snuggling up against him. "Oh, you were so wonderful. God, you were wonderful."

Most men in Renwick's situation would have been quite delighted at these words and at finding Fanny Terrell happily snuggling against them, but Renwick was appalled. Despite the habits of most of the masculine members of his class, he did not often awake to find himself in bed with actresses he scarcely knew. He was a moderate young man and the son of a puritanical father, who had warned him of the sin and vice of London. Indeed, the duke had been reluctant to send him, but had realized he was at an age where he needed a wife. He would find one in London, the duke had said, just as he had found Renwick's mother some thirty-one years before.

"I should be going," said Renwick, starting to get up from the bed.

"Oh Sam," cried Fanny, throwing her arms around him and kissing him on the lips.

The press of Fanny Terrell's voluptuous body against his own prompted Renwick's body to respond accordingly. However, his headache, combined with the thought of the Duke of Welham's dour and disapproving visage, caused his lordship to summon all his self-discipline and pull away gritted his teeth and picked up his clothes, which were ly- as if he had touched a candle flame.

"I've got to be off," he said, extricating himself from her embrace and leaping up from the bed. This exertion caused agonizing pain to shoot through his head, but he ing in disarray on the floor. He dressed quickly, ignoring Mrs. Terrell's pleas to stay "a bit longer."

"No, I must go, Mrs. Terrell," he said weakly.

"Mrs. Terrell? God love me, it was Fanny throughout the night."

"I expect it was, indeed," said his lordship, "but I must be going."

"You're a funny one, Sam Botts."

"Sam Botts—oh, yes, of course. Do forgive me, Fanny, but I must be back to Victor's house."

"Oh, very well." Fanny sat up in bed and pulled the bedclothes across her ample breasts. "If you must go, I suppose you 'ave to, but as soon as this wager's done you'll be back here permanent."

"Permanent?" Renwick buttoned his waistcoat.

"When you're in the troupe. Coo, don't you remember? We talked of nothing else. We'll go far, the two of us."

"Oh, I suppose we will," murmured Renwick, pulling on his coat. "Well, then, I shall be off now, Fanny. And thank you so much."

"Thank me? Oh no, sir. I should be thanking you," cried Fanny, with a raucous laugh. Renwick grimaced. He hastily turned to leave.

"Oh, Sam?"

"Yes."

"You ain't the jealous type, are you?"

"Oh, no, Fanny," he said, a bit too hastily. "Not Sam Botts."

"Good," said Fanny, relieved, althought a bit disappointed. "Come back soon."

"Good day, Fanny," he said hastily, retreating out the door.

Renwick was relieved to be out in the air. The sun was high overhead, and he suspected it was at least noon. He walked down the street several blocks before he realized that he had no idea where he was going, and a quick check of his purse showed that he had no money at all. A query to a passing merchant elicited the general direction of Victor's house, which, according to the helpful merchant, was some three miles distant. The marquis was most grateful and set off toward the fashionable neighborhood where Victor's town house stood.

He walked for several blocks, his head pounding and his

stomach beginning to feel a bit queasy. He continued on his journey, ignoring curious passersby who directed disapproving looks at the rumpled evening clothes and unshaven face that proclaimed him a living example of the dissipation that plagued the city's upper classes.

It was his lordship's great misfortune that, as he continued this miserable and seemingly endless walk, a curricle pulled up beside him and a familiar feminine voice called out, "Lord Renwick!" His lordship stopped and looked up in horror. He knew before he saw the familiar dark eyes and unruly black curls that it was Georgina Suttondale. She was driving the curricle and was accompanied by a stony-faced groom.

"Are you hurt? What is wrong? . . . Sam, do tell me, what is wrong? Have you been robbed?"

"Nothing is wrong, Lady Georgina, I assure you." He felt an unreasonable anger toward her for happening upon him in this disheveled condition, and he was surprised to note the worried expression on her face.

"May I take you to Victor's house? You seem in no condition to walk. It is quite far."

"Oh, I can walk well enough."

"Don't be ridiculous. Get in."

"As you command, m'lady," he replied in a broad north country accent, and got up beside her. She flicked the reins, and the horses were off at a trot.

"You look terrible, my lord," said Georgina.

He was surprised by the "my lord," but realized it was for the benefit of the groom who rode behind them.

"I feel terrible," he said.

"But you are not ill?"

"No, not very."

They rode in silence for some time. He looked over at her, and the thought crossed his mind that had he awakened to find Georgina Suttondale beside him in bed rather than Mrs. Terrell, he would not have left so abruptly. He was immediately ashamed of this thought and irritated with himself for it. "I suppose you think it very uncharacteristic for me to be prowling about the streets at noon dressed like this."

"I had not given too much thought to it."

"You probably worry that it is not at all typical of a marquis and unworthy of my noble birth."

"Indeed not, Sam," replied Georgina, keeping her eyes upon the horses. "It is not at all unusual for gentlemen of rank to come home at noon in such a condition as yours. However, they usually come home in their carriages and are put discreetly to bed by their servants."

"Oh, I see. I shall be more discreet in the future."

Georgina made no reply, and he studied her thoughtfully for a moment. "You think I am disgraceful."

"Your personal conduct is of no consequence to me. Ours is strictly a business arrangement."

"Yes, business."

They were silent again for a time. "Sam," said Georgina, finally.

"My lady?"

"If you wish to end this masquerade, you may do so. I shall pay you the twenty-five pounds in any case."

"And what of your friend's wager? Miss Amesbury will lose three hundred pounds."

Georgina frowned. "I shall attend to that. Don't worry."

"But why would you quit now? I have done very well, haven't I? There is but a week left."

"Oh, I don't know." Georgina pulled the horses up and stopped at the curb. "I don't know if it's right to continue. It was all very well at first, but I am deceiving so many people. You are deceiving so many people."

"You aren't worried about me, are you, my lady?"

"You? Of course not! Why should I be? Do forget I said anything about it. Now please get down. We are three blocks from Victor's house."

"You don't want to be seen with me, then?" Renwick smiled despite his headache.

"I certainly do not. And I suggest you hurry. I do not intend to wait here all day."

Renwick got down from the curricle. He started to say something, but Georgina turned away, and, at the light touch of her whip, the horses continued on their way. Renwick watched her go with a strange mixture of emotions, and then shrugged and turned toward his cousin's house.

9

THE NEWS THAT FANNY TERRELL HAD TAKEN a new lover spread throughout the town with the speed of fresh gossip in a dull season. The news was of great interest to everyone, and the identity of Mrs. Terrell's new protector was of particular interest to two of society's members, Lord Milford and Lady Georgina Suttondale.

Lord Milford was quite outraged to hear that the Marquis of Renwick, so newly arrived from provincial anonymity and, according to his sources, virtually penniless due to his father's stinginess, had gained Mrs. Terrell's favors. Indeed, Lord Milford had been laboring hard to secure that lady's attentions, showering her with expensive trinkets and enduring so many of her performances. It was infamous, thought Milford, that just as he was about to claim his hard-earned reward, a provincial nobody had snatched it from his grasp. The only good thing about the dreadful situation was that he had not already established her as his mistress and few in society knew of his plans to do so. Even so, Milford was furious with Renwick and vowed to do all he could to ensure his failure in society.

Lady Georgina was quite appalled when Penelope whispered the news to her. Her cousin, quite amused, had remarked that Fanny had been quite enamoured of Sam Botts and that he was, after all, a very handsome man.

Georgina, however, saw nothing amusing about the situation and worried for the first time that the masquerade might have unfortunate consequences. Although the Duke of Welham's home was as far from London as one might be and still be in England, it was not impossible that word might reach the duke and the real Marquis of Renwick. Indeed, it might be best if they could conclude this business as quickly as possible.

The other thing that irritated Georgina was that Sam Botts had abused his situation and had, in particular, shown an utter disregard for Victor's well being. It was infuriating, too, that she had chanced upon Botts the morning of the previous day and had unwittingly helped him return from the scene of his assignation. That he would act in such a manner after she had begun to think she had misjudged him was terrible, and she concluded that he was even worse than she had supposed.

Penelope laughed at her cousin's worries and reminded her that they were to go riding and meet Victor in the park. They would also be accompanied by Mrs. Grove, who, although an indifferent horsewoman, had been persuaded to come in order to satisfy Lord Rumbridge's fears that Georgina was not properly chaperoned.

Georgina, Penelope, Mrs. Grove, and a groom set out on this cloudy spring day, Georgina and Penelope, dressed in their fashionable riding habits and mounted upon spirited horses, turned many heads. Georgina was a most accomplished rider and liked nothing better than to ride in the park. However, she was not at all eager to see the erring "Sam Botts" again.

While Georgina rode along thinking ill of Renwick, that gentleman rode beside his cousin Victor. They had arrived early and were waiting for the ladies to arrive.

They walked their mounts leisurely down the path until Victor caught sight of a gentleman astride an enormous black horse coming upon them. Renwick, an accomplished horseman himself, was much impressed by this gentleman's skillful handling of the magnificent black stallion as he pulled the horse up short and hailed them.

"Ballanville, old fellow," called the gentleman. "Been a damned long time since I've seen you."

Victor grinned. "Averton. Good to see you. You remember my cousin, Renwick."

"Of course," said Averton.

A well-known leader of fashion and an intimate of the Prince Regent, Averton was very thin and not particularly handsome, yet his sober, stylish clothes and air of elegant nobility made him stand out among his fellows.

"Fine horse you are riding, sir," said Renwick, looking appreciatively at the animal's shiny black coat and perfectly proportioned limbs.

"Oh yes, Domino is a fine one. Prinny is dashed envious of him. And so, Lord Renwick, I hear that you are already established in the affections of the famous Mrs. Terrell. I must say, that is well done, sir. Mrs. Terrell is all the rage now, and is most particular in her choice of gentlemen. Prinny once said having Fanny Terrell to bed is becoming a prerequisite to attaining a place in elite society."

"Good God," exclaimed Renwick, quite appalled by Averton's frankness. "Don't tell me this has become public knowledge about Mrs. Terrell and me!"

"Don't look so horrified, my lord. As I have said, it is quite an accomplishment."

"Good God," muttered Renwick.

"Oh yes, it is all over town," continued Averton. "Mrs. Terrell was never one to keep secrets. It was a surprise, though, for Brummell and I had thought Milford was to be the next."

"The devil," cried Victor. "Milford and Fanny?"

"My dear Ballanville, it was not yet a *fait accompli*, but poor Milford was trying very hard. Oh look, here come Miss Amesbury and Lady Georgina."

They turned to see the ladies and the groom approaching, and Victor waved to them.

"Hello there," called Penelope. "Marvelous day for riding, although it could rain."

"A few clouds and the threat of rain could not dim the beauty of you ladies," cried Averton melodramatically.

"Such nonsense you talk," said Georgina, "but how good it is to see you and dear Domino."

"Dear Domino is being most difficult today," said Averton, "and bears watching, as do you, Lady Georgina. You look very lovely today."

"Yes, I have missed you, indeed," said Georgina with a smile. "Now what were you gentlemen plotting before we arrived?"

"Plotting?" said Victor. "Mr. Averton was only renewing Renwick's acquaintance."

"Yes, indeed. But, my dear ladies, as much as I should like to stay, I fear I cannot. I must call upon HRH today, and it grows dangerously late. I do insist that all of you come to the party at my house Tuesday night. I have sent invitations a trifle late, as usual, but I have good reason to believe that a certain personage might attend."

"And who might that be?" inquired Renwick.

Georgina looked over at him for the first time. "Do not be ridiculous. Mr. Averton means the prince, of course."

"Indeed, yes, but there's no certainty of it. But I have invited Rumbridge too, and if he is reluctant to go, hint about the prince and he will be certain to accept. Now, good day to all of you." With these final words Averton bounded off on the enormous stallion, leaving Penelope quite excited and stating that she could not wait until Averton's party.

Mrs. Grove, who stared gloomily at them, nodded solemnly at Victor's greeting, and they all proceeded on their way. Penelope was quite thrilled that "Sam Botts" had so easily convinced Averton that he was the Marquis of Renwick, and she informed Georgina and Victor that the bet was as good as won. Victor was sorely tempted to blurt out the truth, but kept silent.

It was not a pleasant ride for Georgina. She found herself riding beside Renwick, and that gentleman's presence was enough to spoil her day. He looked very handsome astride one of Victor's finest horses, and he rode well. In fact Georgina strongly resented his equestrian skill, finding it insolent of Sam Botts that he already seemed to ride like a gentleman.

Victor and Penelope soon grew totally involved with each other, leaving Georgina to talk to Mrs. Grove and Renwick. Since Mrs. Grove's conversation was very limited and since she had no wish to talk to Renwick, Georgina remained uncharacteristically silent.

Renwick was made uncomfortable by her silence, and yet he stubbornly decided that he would not attempt conversation unless Lady Georgina spoke first. Since she had no intention of doing so, they continued on through the park in silence.

The silent ride was interrupted by the appearance of three more riders on the path, two ladies and a gentleman. Renwick recognized the ladies immediately. They were Lady Dunstan and her daughter, Miss Emily. The marquis studied Miss Emily and thought she looked lovely.

Her diminutive form was fashionably garbed in a blue riding habit, and she wore a very fetching hat atop her red-brown curls.

Lady Dunstan greeted them warmly. She was acquainted with all of them and was especially glad to see Renwick again. After meeting him for the first time, she had thought constantly that he would be a good match for Emily. Her elder daughter had married a duke, and she thought it would be quite remarkable to have two duchesses in the family.

Her husband, Lord Dunstan Carlyle, who was riding beside the two ladies, was soon introduced to Renwick, who found him amiable enough. They exchanged a few words and then hurried off. Lady Georgina, who was only slightly acquainted with the Carlyle family, did not fail to notice that little Emily was casting her pretty blue eyes in the direction of Sam Botts. Georgina glanced over at him and noticed with a start that Sam Botts was smiling at Miss Emily.

Perhaps it was her imagination, she thought. Surely he could not forget his place in such an infamous manner. She looked over at him and frowned. Thank God there was only one week left before Lady Carrington's party. Georgina could hardly wait for this event to be over, and then Sam Botts could be sent back to wherever he had come from. It was a stupid, silly wager, thought Georgina and she decided to warn Victor at first opportunity that he had better keep a close watch on this Sam of his, or they may all regret it.

"I say, Hugh," said Victor, carefully adjusting his neck cloth in the mirror. "I think we had best tell Penelope and Georgina about your true identity."

Renwick glanced over at his cousin. "And why is that, Vic? There are only a few days until Lady Carrington's ball. I say we tell them then."

"I don't like it. I told Georgina I would keep you out of sight until the ball."

"You what?"

"She's worried that you'll cause a scandal and ruin my real cousin Renwick's good name. She knows about Fanny Terrell and you."

"She does?"

"Everyone does—even, I suspect, my little cousin Emily."

"Oh, not Emily!" Renwick shook his head. "God, Vic, I don't know what I shall do about Fanny. If the duke hears of it, he shall have my head."

"He shall have mine, is more likely. It is I who has led his virtuous son astray, introducing him to lewd women and drunken revels."

"We have our share of lewd women and drunken revels in the north, Vic."

Victor Ballanville's eyebrows arched in mock horror. "I would never believe it!"

"But what is it that Lady Georgina actually said to you?"

"It was odd, actually. She said that I should take care, that you were a bold fellow. Yes, 'bold fellow' is how she described you, and she said you had forgotten your place. I assured her I would be vigilant. And that is why I do not think we should go to Almack's tonight. Indeed, I think we might as well stay here or go to the club."

"But I have heard so much of Almack's, and I want to go."

"It is always a bore," said Victor but Renwick was unconvinced. He was curious about these elite assembly rooms that only the most privileged could enter.

"Penelope will be there," said Renwick.

"She will not," said Victor. "Penelope refuses to go. She once wheedled a voucher from one of the patronesses, but after attending once, vowed never again. Penelope does not care one fig for the opinion of society, nor does Georgina. I daresay you will not find Georgina there, either, although they dare not exclude her, being sister-in-law to Lady Rumbridge."

Victor's words were in vain, for nothing could sway him from going to Almack's, and Victor reluctantly conceded defeat. Later that evening they found themselves at the assembly rooms, surveying the glittering crowd. Unknown to Victor Ballanville, another person was in reluctant attendance.

Lady Georgina Suttondale stared across the room in disbelief as Victor and his cousin entered. "Of all places to take him!" muttered Georgina.

"What is it, Georgina?"

"Oh nothing, Amelia, it is only that I see Victor Ballanville and . . . another gentleman are here."

"Indeed." Lady Rumbridge looked across the room. "Then the other gentleman is his cousin Lord Renwick."

Georgina did not confirm this, but Amelia nodded. "He is very handsome and very much a gentleman. That is obvious. Really, Georgina, you must cultivate his acquaintance."

"I have no desire to do so," replied Georgina, a trifle too curtly.

Amelia only shook her head. "I cannot understand you at all. But there is my sister. Come, Georgina."

Georgina followed Amelia, but glanced back at Renwick, who, she noted to her great irritation, was already talking to none other than Lady Dunstan Carlyle. Dolllike Emily was standing beside her mother, looking up at him with wide eyes. Georgina was furious. Had she been a man, she would have thrashed the impudent Sam Botts soundly.

However, being a member of the gentler sex, Georgina could only clench her fists and follow Lady Rumbridge, and wait until she had the opportunity to talk to Victor Ballanville. This opportunity arrived shortly, when that gentleman passed by and, seeing Georgina, stopped and greeted her.

"Lady Georgina," he said formally, since her sister-in-law was standing beside her. "I had no idea that you were in attendance. And Lady Rumbridge. How good to see you, ma'am."

Lady Rumbridge nodded to him condescendingly and turned to talk to another lady.

"It is quite evident, Mr. Ballanville," said Georgina, "that you did not know I would be here. Oh, Victor, I am so angry with you!"

"Georgina, if it's about my—that is to say Sam Botts, I must assure you that you have no cause to worry. I have no fears that he will do anything that would disgrace Renwick."

As they talked, the orchestra began to play a waltz, and Georgina looked over at the dancers. Prominent among the swirling couples was the tall form of Renwick, and in his arms was the diminutive Miss Emily, her face flushed with excitement as she gazed shyly into his face. What was even more infuriating than this sight in itself was the fact that Renwick was dancing about the room without a trace of the clumsiness he had shown when, only a few days earlier, she had tried to teach him to dance.

"Look at that, Victor. Why, your Sam Botts is waltzing! Oh, I should love to murder the fellow! I daresay he was able to dance all the time and feigned clumsiness to vex me."

"Oh, surely not," said Victor. "It is only that he has caught on finally."

"Oh, Victor!"

"Georgina, please do not be angry. I must explain. Yes, I think this has all gone far enough."

"And what has gone far enough?" Lady Rumbridge had returned and had entered the conversation suddenly.

"Oh, nothing, Lady Rumbridge. Pray, excuse me."

He retreated hastily, and Georgina frowned.

"How very odd," commented the countess. "But I never cared very much for Mr. Ballanville. He is a very unsteady young man and a fortune hunter."

It was a great surprise to Lady Rumbridge that her sister-in-law made no effort to defend Victor Ballanville. Instead, Georgina said that she had a headache and hoped that they would leave soon.

The Marquis of Renwick had thought Miss Emily Carlyle one of the most enchanting ladies he had ever met. She was so delicate, and delightfully feminine. However, his lordship was not entirely blinded by Miss Emily's charms; he soon noted that she had an unfortunate tendency to prattle. She had been shy at first, but seemed to overcome this characteristic very quickly and soon began talking rapidly in a high-pitched, childish voice.

Many men found Miss Emily's prattle one of her most endearing characteristics, but Renwick soon discovered that she possessed not one ounce of wit and her conversation was limited to an unending babble about her new gowns and the activities of a mischievous lapdog named Puck.

"Puck is adorable," squeaked Miss Emily as they danced. "You would love him, my lord. Just today as I was going out, my darling Puck was very naughty. He jumped from my arms and rushed across the street and I was so very worried." Miss Emily's face took on a perplexed expression. "I don't know why he would have done such a thing, but Harry soon fetched him back and I knew he was very sorry, for he looked so very sad and funny and who could be angry with him when he is so adorable?"

"Who, indeed?" said his lordship, who was beginning to find Miss Emily's company quite tedious. These were the only words he had the opportunity to say, for Miss Emily chattered on about Puck until Renwick finally was able to break away from her. Leaving the lovely Miss Emily with her mother and several ardent suitors, he retreated across the room.

Lady Georgina had been sipping a glass of punch and waiting impatiently for her sister-in-law to conclude her good-byes so that they might leave. She had watched Renwick with Emily Carlyle and had been so angered by the sight that she doubted she could be civil to Sam Botts had she the misfortune to meet up with him.

Therefore, when she saw him leave Miss Emily and come walking in her direction, she turned away and tried to be inconspicuous.

"Lady Georgina."

"Sir," she said coldly.

"I did not know you were here."

"Indeed."

He was surprised and irritated by her undisguised disdain.

"You seem in a devil of a mood, my lady."

"Do I, *my lord?*" she said sarcastically. "I advise you to leave me, sir, for it is you who have brought about this mood."

"I?"

"You disgust me!"

He had not expected such a violent response and regarded her in surprise.

"You, Sam Botts, are the most despicable man. How dare you make up to a lady like Emily Carlyle! It is bad enough that you carry on with Fanny Terrell! But now you toy with a young lady's affections, allowing her to believe you are a gentleman. It is too much, sir. What will happen when she finds out who you are? Indeed, I do not think she will find the footman Sam Botts so very interesting. May I remind you, sir, that your charm, if indeed she finds you charming, lies only in your supposed rank and fortune. And stripped of these, as you soon shall be, there is little left."

Renwick's face grew dark. "Is that so, my lady?" he said, and his voice was so cold and terrible that Georgina was alarmed. "And I suppose if your precious rank were gone, you would still be a great lady of society! I think not, madam."

She could not reply, but hurried away before she would burst into tears or scream at him. Renwick watched her go, and, angry as he was, he regretted his words. He had lied. He did not doubt that had she been born to poverty, she would still have been an extraordinary lady.

Two days after her miserable evening at Almack's, Georgina went to call upon Penelope Amesbury. As always, her cousin was overjoyed to see her, acting as if they had been separated for weeks rather than a mere two days. For once Penelope's house was empty. Mr. Falconrest had finished his portrait, a very successful painting that was displayed prominently on the wall, and the rest of Penelope's usual visitors had evidently had other commitments.

Georgina was glad to see this, for she wished to talk to her cousin privately and was soon launched into a description of Sam Botts's behavior. She declared that Victor did not fully realize that his servant was a treacherous rogue. Penelope listened sympathetically, but was unable to become upset about the matter, insisting that Sam was only having "a bit of fun" and that the "poor fellow" may as well enjoy his brief experience as a noble lord in the few days remaining.

This comment was hardly what Georgina wished to hear, but rather than argue with her beloved cousin, she changed the subject, expressing a wish to see the little mare that they had rescued from the hands of her cruel master. Penelope was not eager to visit the stables, but had no objection to Georgina's doing so, and Georgina left the house to see how the poor creature was faring.

She had just left the room when the door bell sounded. Penelope's butler announced the arrival of the Marquis of Renwick and Mr. Ballanville. As always, Penelope was overjoyed to see her darling Victor. After kissing him happily, she turned to Renwick.

"Oh dear, Sam, you have certainly displeased Georgina. She thinks you terrible! She tells me that you were mooning about Emily Carlyle at Almack's, and although I can hardly picture you 'mooning' about anyone, I too think it terrible—though perhaps for different reasons. Emily Carlyle is a little ninny, after all. Indeed, I can well understand your being taken with Fanny. She is quite the fashion; but Emily!"

Renwick did not like to hear any mention of Fanny Terrell. She had been sending him notes, written in her flamboyant hand, that were most indiscreet and appallingly graphic. The marquis's sober replies, in which he hinted it would be best to break off the affair, only induced Fanny to write again, pleading that he come to her and discuss the matter. Although Victor found this all very amusing, Renwick did not, and wished that he had never met Fanny.

"But there is not much time left until Lady Carrington's ball, and then we shall have done with this," continue Penelope. "I know Georgina is most anxious to conclude this wager, but I think it has all been very amusing."

"I had thought we might find Georgina here," remarked Victor.

"Oh, she is here. She went to the stables to see her horse. You remember the poor nag that Georgina and Sam were so concerned about?"

"I could not easily forget that episode," said Victor.

Renwick looked thoughtful. "I should like to see the horse, if I may."

"Splendid idea, Sam, and apologize to Lady Georgina in the process." Victor smiled. "Miss Amesbury and I can spare your company."

Renwick left his cousin and Penelope, who were always eager for moments alone, and entered the stable. He noted first Penelope's carriage horses and then spotted Georgina. She was standing beside the little roan mare, talking softly to the animal and patting her fondly.

"She's much improved, I see."

Georgina was startled by his voice and turned to face him. "Oh, you."

"Yes, 'tis I."

Georgina turned back to the horse. "I don't wish to talk to you. I pray you leave me."

Renwick ignored this comment and patted the horse. "She's looking much better, and she's not a bad-looking little creature now that she's rested." His expert eye traveled appraisingly over the mare. "No, she's a fair enough little horse. Have you given her a name?"

She hesitated, for she had no wish to be civil, but finally replied, "Matilda."

"Matilda," he repeated. "A good enough name, I suppose. I have an aunt Matilda."

Georgina was ignoring him, and he glanced over at her. She was frowning and taking care not to look in his direction. They both were silent for a time, and finally Renwick spoke. "I want to apologize for what I said to you that evening at Almack's."

She continued to pat the little mare.

"No matter how angry you made me, I had no right to talk to you in such a manner."

"I made *you* angry?" She looked over at him for the first time. "If you recall, Sam Botts, it was you who seemed to forget yourself dancing with Miss Emily Carlyle—and dancing very well, I might add. But perhaps that was due to your partner, who was not a plowhorse like myself."

Her indignant expression and the memory of the time when they had danced caused the marquis to burst into laughter. She cast him a withering look and began to walk angrily away.

"Wait! Please," he said, regretting his laughter. "I *do* want to apologize. And you have no need worry about poor Miss Emily. I won't dance with her again, I assure you. I am not enamoured of her in the least."

"She shall be terribly crushed to hear that, Sam Botts. By my honor, your impudence is beyond belief! I don't want your apologies or your explanations. I only want you to keep away from me, and after this unfortunate business of the Carrington ball has ended, I wish never to see your insolent face again."

She gave him no opportunity for reply, but rushed back to the house and, saying a quick good-bye to Penelope and Victor, returned home.

Renwick remained in the stable for a while. "You've a difficult mistress, Matilda," he said, looking again at the little roan mare. "But it's I who am the fool. I should have told her the truth long ago. By God, I would have done so today if she had given me the opportunity."

Matilda regarded him with her brown eyes and twitched her ears. Renwick frowned. "She's the most infuriating female. I pray God she soon finds a husband who'll take her in hand." However, this comment only brought to mind the Viscount Milford; and for some inexplicable reason the thought of Milford or any other gentleman taking the wayward Lady Georgina to wife did not at all please him. "Damn," he muttered, and, giving Matilda one last pat, left the stable.

10

DINNER THAT EVENING WITH HER BROTHER AND sister-in-law was a trial for Georgina. It was difficult to appreciate the excellent roast lamb and savory puddings when faced with the Countess of Rumbridge's disapproving gaze. Lady Rumbridge was more than usually quiet that night, and although Georgina did not know the reason for her sister-in-law's ill humor, she suspected it had something to do with her.

Actually, the countess was disappointed by a rumor she had heard that afternoon about the Marquis of Renwick and Mrs. Terrell. Her dearest wish was that Georgina get married and leave their household, and she had thought Lord Renwick a likely suitor. However, his affair with Mrs. Terrell made him quite unacceptable to Rumbridge. Of course, the earl had been quite optimistic that Lord Milford might make an offer, and Lady Rumbridge hoped desperately that he would act soon.

Georgina had hoped that her brother might mention Richard Averton's invitation, but when he failed to do so after two days of repeated hints about "busy social schedules" and "numerous parties and balls," Georgina was forced to ask him at dinner. "Did you receive Mr. Averton's invitation for tomorrow?"

The countess sniffed. "Imagine that man sending these hastily scribbled notes and expecting people of quality to come running."

"Indeed," said the Earl. "You know my feelings about Richard Averton. He is a lowborn upstart, and I shall not accept invitations from him."

"But Robert, the prince will be there."

"The prince?" The countess was suddenly interested. "Perhaps if the prince were going to be there—"

"Now, Amelia," interrupted the earl. "I am not so blinded by the prince's rank to be unaware of his shocking behavior. He has brought dishonor to the royal family, and I do not intend to fawn over him. His behavior to the Princess of Wales is unforgivable, and regent and heir to the throne or no, His Royal Highness is not fit company for my wife or my sister."

Georgina thought she detected a trace of disappointment on the countess's face, but she saw immediately that there was no point in arguing with her brother. It was abominable to miss Richard's party, which would certainly be one of the most amusing affairs of the season. Georgina looked again at her sister-in-law, hoping that Amelia might convince Rumbridge to change his mind.

"I do think I will retire early this evening," said Georgina, hoping to retreat before she got into an argument. Her brother made no objection, and she retired to her room and to the pages of a romantic novel.

The following day Georgina dutifully accompanied Amelia on her morning calls. Surprisingly, the calls were quite pleasant, and Georgina and Amelia returned on remarkably good terms. It was noon, and they found Rumbridge awaiting their arrival, a look of anticipation on his face.

They had barely time to take off their bonnets before Rumbridge was urging them both to be seated upon the sofa. "I have good news for you. I have had visitors this morning. Quite unexpected, and I have received two offers for Georgina's hand."

"How marvelous," said Amelia. "Pray tell us who has called."

"The first caller I hesitate to mention. I was rather shocked that he should have the audacity to believe I might even consider his proposal."

"Indeed?" said Georgina, having no idea whom he could be speaking of.

"Who was it, Robert?"

"Sir Swithin Baxter."

"Baxter?" Lady Rumbridge's mouth dropped open, and Georgina burst into gales of laughter.

"Swithin?" she finally managed to say. "It is too funny."

"It is scandalous! That old debauchee. Really, Georgina, you should not be encouraging him."

"I am not encouraging him, Amelia. I have not seen him in ages, and I must say I am quite dumbfounded. Surely he is joking."

"He is not. He was accompanied by his solicitor, a highly respected man, and he was most specific in matters of finance. Baxter is a fool, but he was willing to be very generous. He has no heirs, and should there be no children all his property would be settled on Georgina."

"Children?" said the countess, quite shocked. "Why, Sir Swithin is at least seventy."

"Yet he did not rule out the possibility," said Rumbridge a trifle sheepishly, and Georgina laughed.

"Swithin? I would never have imagined he could be serious," she said.

"You mean he's mentioned this to you?"

"Only in jest, Amelia. Or I thought it was only in jest. Hmmm . . . Lady Baxter. It is not a bad-sounding name is it?"

"Surely you are not considering it?" cried Amelia.

"A sensible lady considers all the possibilities," said Georgina mischievously.

"That is true," said Rumbridge seriously, "but I ruled out Baxter, and told him so. It was out of the question. And I was glad I told him so, for no sooner had Baxter left than who should appear but Lord Milford."

"Oh, that's wonderful," cried the countess.

"What do you think, Georgina? I was quite encouraging to Milford. I have always thought him the man for you. Perhaps he is not as wealthy as I might hope, but his fortune is quite sufficient."

Georgina frowned. "You know how I feel about Lord Milford. I do not wish to marry him. Indeed, I should marry almost anyone over him."

"But Georgina," said the countess. "He is perfect for you, and my dear . . ." She paused. "I do not like to say this, but I must make this observation. You are nearly three and twenty, and although deluged with proposals in your first season (all of which I am told you heartlessly spurned), you have received no offers for a year. My dear

Georgina, these offers may be the only ones you will receive."

Georgina stared resentfully at her sister-in-law. "You are probably right, Amelia, but nothing could induce me to marry Milford. If forced to choose between the two offers, I would quickly pick Sir Swithin."

"You are impossible," muttered the countess.

Before Rumbridge could say anything, the butler arrived to announce Miss Amesbury and Mrs. Grove. "Of all times for her to come," said the earl. "I am in no mood to see Penelope now."

"But I wish to see her."

"Very well, Georgina, but you will see her alone. Amelia and I will leave you. Discuss the matter with your cousin and perhaps you will see things more clearly."

The countess looked doubtfully at her husband and then followed him from the drawing room. Moments later Penelope entered, dressed in a splendid new outfit of mauve silk and a remarkable hat covered with plumes. She was followed by Mrs. Grove.

"Oh, coz," said Penelope, embracing Georgina. "You do not appear very happy, and you were quite unhappy yesterday, too. My poor dear, it does not suit you to be so glum."

After greeting Mrs. Grove and having the ladies sit down, Georgina began her tale of the marriage proposals. At the mention of Swithin Baxter's name, Penelope let out a most unladylike, "The devil!" On hearing of Milford's offer, she shook her head.

"My poor darling Georgie. What sort of choice is that to make? Pity Sam Botts is not really Renwick and that he doesn't make you an offer."

"That is absurd, Penelope. And I should not like him if he were a prince of the blood."

"Well, Fanny likes him, it seems, and she knows he's only Sam Botts. But he's so dreadfully handsome that I can understand why Fanny is so taken with him. But coz, what will you do? It is obvious you cannot marry Milford. He is odious, for one thing, and another thing is that the prince is certain to drop him very soon and he is very little without Prinny's patronage."

"He is very little with it."

"Indeed, yes. But then there are only two other choices

—marry Swithin or remain as you are and await other offers."

"It is growing very difficult to remain as I am. Amelia is becoming more unbearable each day. If I reject Milford, she will be intolerable."

"Then you must come and live with Victor and me once we are married."

"Oh Penelope, Rumbridge would never stand for that."

"I suppose not. Then you must marry Swithin. Oh, it is a repugnant idea, but perhaps it would not be so bad. Swithin dotes on you, and he is very rich. Pity he is such an idiot. But he is very liberal about certain things and would leave you to amuse yourself as you wish."

"Penelope!"

"Do not shriek at me, my dear prudish cousin. It is very well to be faithful to one's husband if one's husband is Victor Ballanville. Victor is an adorable darling, and I am so desperately in love with him that I should never look twice at another man. But if one were to marry Swithin Baxter, one could be forgiven for seeking solace with handsome fellows who look like Sam Botts."

"Penelope, do cease this shocking talk. I have no intention to marry Swithin—although I almost considered the idea, if only to spite Rumbridge. I will marry no one and that is final."

"Good. At least until we find you someone you like. Swithin? Oh dear. And he never said a word about it to anyone! Oh, wait until I tell Victor."

"You will not tell him, Penelope. I beg you!"

"Oh, very well. But it would be so amusing to tell everyone. HRH would be so amused. That reminds me, coz. I have word from Victor that HRH will be at Richard Averton's party, so we must look our best. I do hope Rumbridge and Amelia will not be too stuffy."

"They are not attending."

"What?"

"No, and Rumbridge has forbidden me to go."

"Oh no, Georgie!"

"Do not fear. I am going in any case. Rumbridge is mistaken if he believes he can tell me what I can do and whom I must marry. You must come round here for me at ten."

"But Rumbridge?"

"He won't be here. They are attending another party at Amelia's sister's house. I will complain of a headache and stay here."

Mrs. Grove listened to this conversation without much interest, but frowned at Georgina's last remark and looked over at Penelope.

"Oh Mrs. Grove, don't be a wet fish," laughed Penelope, patting that woman's arm. Mrs. Grove only frowned more deeply.

"We shall be here for you promptly at ten. Oh, it shall be such fun. And do reconsider allowing me to tell Prinny about Swithin. Oh, very well, I shall be as discreet as anyone can be. Good day, dear coz. Until tonight, then."

With Mrs. Grove in tow, Penelope hurried out, leaving Georgina to sit down upon the sofa and feel quite depressed.

Despite her reputation as an adventuresome and rather wild young lady, Lady Georgina Suttondale did have some misgivings about sneaking off to the party at Richard Averton's house. Yet her resentment toward her brother was so strong that she decided to carry out her plan. As soon as Rumbridge and the countess were safely out of the way, Georgina astonished her maid, Sally, by ordering her to bring out her best evening gown.

There was little time, and Georgina fidgeted while Sally fixed her hair, carefully adorning her coiffure with splendid ostrich plumes. A quick glance in the mirror assured Georgina that she had never looked better, and she hastily rushed downstairs as the mantel clock chimed the hour of ten.

A footman met her at the door and escorted her to the carriage where Victor, Penelope, Renwick, and the disagreeable Mrs. Grove awaited her arrival.

"How lovely you look, coz," said Penelope.

"Indeed, yes," said Victor. "But we all look splendid tonight, even poor old Sam here."

Georgina had taken a place next to Penelope, and opposite her, beside Mrs. Grove, sat Renwick. He looked infuriatingly handsome, his blue eyes regarding her with an intent expression that made her very uncomfortable. However, she tried to act as if he were not even there.

"I was not certain that we should bring Sam tonight,

Georgina. After all, the prince will be there, and I daresay I do not relish the idea of misleading HRH. But Victor insists that it will be fine."

Victor nodded. "Yes, have no fear, for I assure you that old Sam will act just as my cousin Renwick would act. And HRH will never know anything about it."

"You realize that I disapprove, Victor," said Georgina coldly. "I would think it wiser for Sam to stay away from society until the ball. It is folly to risk discovery like this when the prince will be in attendance."

"There is nothing to worry about," said Victor. "And Sam needs more practice, don't you, Sam?"

Renwick grinned at Georgina. "Aye, that I do, but never fear, my lady, as Mr. Ballanville says I'll be acting just like his lordship. Seems I know him as I know myself by now." He smiled again, and Georgina frowned warningly in return.

Dressed in his impeccably tailored evening suit, Richard Averton was a magnificent sight. He awaited his guests with a cultivated expression of ennui and looked upon his first arrival, Lord Milford, without much enthusiasm.

"Milford, you are first to arrive."

"Am I, Averton? I should have known no one would come very early." Milford, too, was dressed in a close-fitting evening suit of elegant black. Brummell had made the look fashionable, and although Milford did miss the splendid satins and velvets of the old days, he had to admit that he himself looked very well in black.

"It is a dull season, is it not, Averton?"

"Is it? Perhaps you are right, although this news of Fanny Terrell is amusing."

"News?" said Milford, hoping to sound nonchalant.

"Surely you have heard she has found a new gentleman? Everyone has been talking about it for days now. The lucky fellow is just come to town. He's the Marquis of Renwick, cousin to Victor Ballanville. Everyone is so eager to meet him, and I am happy to say that he will be here tonight."

Lord Milford looked none too pleased by this news. "I have already met the gentleman, and frankly, I fear poor Fanny's taste is not what it once was. This Renwick is rather unpolished and hopelessly provincial."

Averton smiled a funny little smile. "I did not find him so at all. Ah, someone else has arrived." The butler announced in very somber tones the arrival of Mr. and Mrs. Terrell.

Mr. Terrell was a stout man many years older than his wife. He was a jolly, likable man who was well tolerated, although little noticed, in society, and he gladly allowed his wife to take center stage whenever they appeared together. He was also remarkably open-minded about Fanny's extramarital affairs, and his great tolerance was linked to his wife's generosity in sharing with him the money and jewels that happened her way.

"Dear Mrs. Terrell, how beautiful you look."

Fanny took Richard Averton's hand. "My dear Mr. Averton, and Lord Milford."

Milford scowled at her, but she only smiled and raised her gloved hand to her throat. Milford's eyes followed the gesture, and he nearly lost his composure to see that she was wearing an exquisite diamond necklace, one that he had given her two weeks before.

He was stunned and angry, but managed to regard her dispassionately while the butler announced the arrival of the Marquis of Renwick, Lady Georgina, Penelope, Victor, and Mrs. Grove.

"Ah, how wonderful to see you all," said Averton genuinely. "I believe everyone knows everyone, or mostly everyone."

The guests, with the exception of Milford, nodded amiably at each other as the butler announced a Lord and Lady Edgemont and a Mr. and Mrs. Cottingham-Smithers. This completed Richard Averton's guest list save for the prince, and everyone stood about, waiting for him to arrive.

Georgina was growing very hungry and commented that she hoped His Royal Highness might arrive before she starved. As if on cue, George, Prince of Wales, entered, followed by two of his aides. All those present made their bows as the prince entered and made his way over to Averton.

"Good evening, Dick."

"How good of Your Royal Highness to come."

While the prince addressed his host, Renwick had ample opportunity to study his prince. He had recently reached his fiftieth birthday, and he had grown quite stout, yet he was still impressive, grandly dressed and with a princely bearing that left no doubt he was the first gentleman of the land.

The prince was at his most charming that evening, and he walked about the room, addressing each of the guests. All save Renwick were known to him, and he asked Averton to introduce him. Georgina was slightly nervous as Renwick approached the prince, but she soon saw that he acted with great aplomb, treating the prince with the proper amount of deference and conducting himself very well indeed. It was soon clear that the prince was most impressed with the young marquis, a fact that for some reason irritated Georgina. She and Lady Edgemont, being the two highest-ranking ladies, had the enviable privilege of sitting next to His Royal Highness at supper.

Fanny Terrell would have enjoyed such an honor, but gained comfort from the fact that she was seated beside Sam Botts, who to Fanny's mind looked very much like the marquis he was pretending to be. Renwick tried to disguise his discomfort at finding himself beside Mrs. Terrell. She was dressed in a most daring gown of filmy material that bared a great deal of her considerable charms, and Renwick found her breathtakingly low décolletage was making it difficult to concentrate on his supper. Even more disconcertingly, Mrs. Terrell directed throaty whispers to him and surreptitiously squeezed his leg from underneath the table.

Although it was difficult to ignore the indelicate suggestions that Mrs. Terrell was whispering to him, Renwick found himself gazing at the Prince Regent and Georgina. He had not failed to notice how beautiful she looked as she entered the carriage that night, and he did not blame the prince for his rapt attentiveness to her.

Mrs. Terrell noted his gaze and frowned. "Is it Lady Georgina that's got you so mystified?" she said.

"Why, Mrs. Terrell, certainly not. It is not every day that I see the Prince Regent. Hard to believe he is actually here."

Although Fanny had not thought Renwick the sort to fawn over royalty, she accepted his explanation and smiled fondly at him. "You have been hard on me, Sam, staying away so long and sending me that dreadful letter. I knew you didn't mean it."

"But Mrs. Terrell, that is to say Fanny, . . ."

The lady leaned toward him with a knowing smile, and he continued with considerable difficulty. "We must not talk of this here. Later, perhaps. Tomorrow would be better."

"I shall be waiting," replied Fanny in a soft voice that utterly disconcerted him.

He desperately hoped that no one had been watching him, for he knew his face was reddening and he looked very much like a schoolboy. Unknown to the marquis, only one of the dinner guests had been watching him. Although occupied with the prince, Lady Georgina had glanced in his direction and was appalled by his behavior. Georgina did not think he looked at all like a schoolboy. She thought he looked very much like a shameless rake, and she was quite disgusted by the way he returned Mrs. Terrell's lustful gaze.

Renwick was glad when the supper ended and the ladies retired to the drawing room. However, the prince was soon eager to rejoin them, and the gentlemen did not linger over their wine.

The guests soon divided up to play cards, and Georgina, Penelope, and Victor ended up at the prince's table, while Renwick found himself once again beside Mrs. Terrell. Her presence made it difficult for him to think about his cards, and since he was rather inexperienced at cards (the duke strongly disapproved of gaming), he lost badly to Lord Edgemont and Fanny. Lord Milford remained apart from the card playing and stared grimly at Fanny Terrell and Renwick. After giving up his chair to Mr. Cottingham-Smithers, Renwick left the card game and retreated to the far side of the room. Here he turned his attention upon Georgina and the prince.

Lady Georgina appeared to be enjoying herself, as did His Royal Highness, who was laughing heartily as he turned from Georgina to Penelope and then back to Georgina. She seemed to be doing well with her cards, and Renwick frowned at the way she looked at the prince. He had heard much about the Prince Regent's lack of scruples where women were concerned, and he did not approve of young unmarried ladies, and especially Lady Georgina, acting so casually with him.

"Lord Renwick." Renwick's thoughts were interrupted by Milford.

"Milford."

"You have risen very fast, it seems," said the viscount. "Only just arrived from the country and already in such company. But let me tell you, sir, I do not much like your conduct with Mrs. Terrell."

Renwick made no reply.

"I suppose she thinks an heir to a dukedom better sport than a mere viscount, but I wonder if she knows your father holds tightly to your purse strings."

This comment brought a smile to Renwick's face. "I know for a fact, sir, that my rank means nothing to Mrs. Terrell. I fear, Milford, that it is the man and not the rank that interests the lady."

"You insolent puppy," sputtered Milford.

"You pompous overbearing fool," replied Renwick, the Ballanville temper thoroughly aroused.

"How dare you, sir?" cried Milford in a loud voice, and all the guests turned toward him. "I should teach you some manners, bumpkin. You will not insult me with impunity."

It was evident to Renwick that Milford was about to issue a challenge, and in his infuriated state, Renwick was eager to accept. However, he did not have the opportunity, for an angry Prince of Wales stopped the argument by appearing beside them and glowering threateningly.

"Gentlemen," he said sternly. "May I remind you that there are ladies present and that you are behaving in a disgraceful manner, raising your voices like fishwives!"

"I am sorry, Your Royal Highness," said Renwick, thoroughly ashamed and yet still furious.

"I, too, sir," said Milford a trifle grudgingly.

"Good," said the prince, who abhorred unpleasantness. "Shake hands and act like gentlemen." They did as he commanded, but exchanged malevolent looks that, fortunately, were undetected by Prince George. His Royal Highness, satisfied with his role of peacemaker, nodded curtly to them and rejoined the ladies. Renwick noted that all eyes were still upon them and that the Lady Georgina was regarding him with an expression of dismay. "Damn," thought Renwick, quickly eluding her gaze. He then caught Fanny Terrell's eye and saw that she was staring at him with a knowing and affectionate smile.

"How could you cause such a scene?" Lady Georgina glared at Renwick from her seat in the carriage. "To be publicly reprimanded by the prince is disgraceful."

"Do calm down," said Penelope. "HRH knows that it was Milford's fault."

"Indeed, yes," added Victor. "Prinny is well aware that Milford is an ass. Do not blame Renwick—or, I should say Sam."

Renwick was staring sullenly at Georgina, and she shook her head. "I was an idiot for believing you could ever act like a gentleman. In addition to your outburst with Milford, I found it sickening how you flirted with Mrs. Terrell all evening."

"Sickening, was it?" Renwick spoke for the first time. "And I suppose you think it fine the way you conducted yourself throughout the evening, fawning about the prince and hanging on his every word. I saw you turning those big brown eyes of yours upon him with such looks of tender regard."

"You forget yourself!" cried Georgina, suddenly outraged. "You dare to criticize my conduct! I will not have it, Sam Botts! This stupid wager is off! I shall have nothing more to do with you!"

"Oh Georgie! You can't mean it!" Penelope was alarmed by her cousin's fury. She had never seen Georgina so angry. Indeed, it was Georgina who was always admonishing her to mind her temper. "This is all ridiculous. It seemed to me that it was Mrs. Terrell who flirted with Sam; and, Sam, it is the duty of every patriotic woman to flirt with the prince. You are both acting like children. It would be foolish to end the contest when the bet is so nearly won. Oh, please reconsider, Georgie!"

"I will not," said Georgina. "I never want to see this person again in the guise of a gentleman, or indeed in any guise at all."

"Wait, Georgina," said Victor, "I think it is time I told you about Sam, as you call him. He is really—"

"*Mr.* Ballanville!" Renwick gave his cousin a warning look, and Victor hesitated.

"What is it, Victor?" said Penelope.

Victor looked again at Renwick and shrugged. "Nothing, nothing at all."

Georgina frowned. "Do not try and defend him, Victor." Victor looked helplessly at Penelope as Georgina and Renwick eyed each other with murderous expressions.

The mantel clock was just striking four when Georgina entered the house and quietly made her way to the stairs. No one was about, and Georgina hoped desperately that her arrival would be undetected. This hope was quickly dashed when a masculine voice startled her.

"So there you are, miss."

"Oh, Robert, you scared me so." Georgina turned at the base of the stairs to face the Earl of Rumbridge, attired in his dressing gown and carrying a candle.

"I waited for you. I've been here for nearly two hours, and I demand to know where you have been."

"Robert, I am in no mood for interrogations."

"Where have you been?" repeated the earl in an even but decidedly angry voice.

"Oh, very well. I was at Richard Averton's house. I know you forbade me to go, Robert, but I was angry. Do not glare at me so. It was quite respectable!"

"Respectable, was it? My dear sister, you do not seem to share my ideas concerning respectability. Is it respectable for an unmarried female to dash about unescorted to the home of a man I detest? I suppose you were accompanied by cousin Penelope and that fool Ballanville!" Rumbridge's face grew hard and terrible in the flickering candlelight. "I will not have you disgracing me or the family name. My sons will not have an aunt who is notorious and who runs about town with no regard for her virtue—thank God that at least they are both away at school. No, my dear sister, I will not have scandal mar this house. You are under my authority, and, by God, you will do as I bid you!

"You will go nowhere without my permission. You shall have no guests unless I approve of them. You shall not see Penelope Amesbury until her wedding."

"But that is three weeks away! Oh, Robert!"

The earl grasped her roughly by the arm. "I have been too lenient with you, my girl. I see that now. But no longer! Your every move will be watched, and I shall take every measure to make certain you do not disgrace me. Now get to your room, and you will do well to think on your unfortunate behavior."

Georgina pulled her arm free and gazed at him in horror-stricken silence. Then, bursting into tears, she ran up the stairs and into her room and threw herself upon the bed.

11

"OH, MY LADY!"

Georgina awoke to find Sally standing over her with a worried expression upon her face. "Oh, Sally." Georgina looked around and realized with a start that she was still wearing her evening gown and the ostrich plumes that decorated her hair were flopping down ludicrously at the side of her head. "What time is it?"

"Noon, my lady. I did try to wake your ladyship earlier, but you were very tired. I had waited for you, my lady, but his lordship instructed me to go to bed."

"Oh, don't worry, Sally. I am all right." Georgina got up from the bed and glanced over at the mirror. "I look a sight, and fear I have ruined this poor dress. Oh, Sally, I believe I have had the worst night of my life."

"Your bath is ready, my lady."

"My bath? Oh, dear Sally, you are an angel!"

Sally grinned at her mistress and began to undress her. When Georgina had sunk wearily into the elegant enameled bath, she sat reflecting upon the previous evening. Why had she allowed Sam Botts to upset her so? After all, he was a common ruffian, and she a lady. Georgina smiled ruefully. A lady? To Rumbridge she was a wayward child.

The thought of her meeting with her brother angered her. He was abominable, but the unfortunate fact was that he did have authority over her. The injustice of the situation grated upon her, and she knitted her brows in concentration. What could she do? She had no money of her own, nor did she have anyone else to whom she could turn save Penelope, and Rumbridge had forbidden her to see her cousin.

These dismal thoughts came close to reducing Lady Georgina to tears, but, summoning all her courage, she rose from the bath and resolved to dress and plead with Robert. Perhaps he would be more reasonable that day.

Sally helped her to dress and, just as she was combing Georgina's dark hair, there was a knock at the door and Lady Rumbridge's maid entered, bearing a note from the earl. The note, written in Rumbridge's angular hand, showed no evidence of a lessening of hostilities. Indeed, the earl expressed hope that Georgina had "repented of her willful behavior" and stated that she was "required" to stay in her room to "reflect upon her duty." This missive did not do much to improve Georgina's mood, and she crumpled the note and threw it to the floor.

"I am a prisoner, it seems, Sally," said Georgina bitterly. "A prisoner." Sally looked sympathetically at her mistress. "I will not stand for this treatment, Sally." Georgina looked thoughtful for a moment. "Is his lordship downstairs?"

"No, my lady," said Sally. "He and her ladyship have gone to pay a call."

"Have they? Well, I am going out. I'll not stay here any longer."

Georgina's steely resolve was greatly admired by Sally, who hastened to ready her mistress to go out. Georgina, now attired in one of her fashionable walking dresses and matching pelisse, made her way downstairs and to the front door. However, Georgina had not reckoned on her brother's determination. As she hurried to the door, a footman barred her way.

Georgina was astonished. "Jim, please get out of my way."

The young man looked apologetic, but made no move from his position in front of the door. "Forgive me, m'lady, but I have orders. Your ladyship must stay in the house. 'Tis the master's orders. I'm dreadful sorry, m'lady."

"Stand aside, Jim!"

"Please, m'lady," replied the servant. "I cannot."

Georgina looked at the young man's pained expression. He appeared sympathetic, but unyielding. Georgina managed a dignified, "Very well," and walked haughtily back upstairs. Once inside her room, she muttered a most unladylike "Damnation!" and kicked an unwary footstool, which went clattering out of her way. "A prisoner!" she cried.

Sally was very upset, but could do nothing to comfort Lady Georgina.

"So he is having me watched, is he?"

"Aye, my lady. Jim is at the front and Amos is at the back, and Mr. Perkins is out watching the street."

"Infamous!" Georgina rushed to the window and saw a tall man in a cloak watching the house. "Yes, there is Perkins. How could Rumbridge do this to me? By my honor, Sally, I'll not be penned like an animal!"

Sally looked very uncomfortable. She loved her mistress dearly, but knew the look that now appeared in Georgina's dark eyes could mean only trouble.

"I am treated like a criminal, so I shall act like one. I shall steal from the house without anyone seeing me."

"Oh, my lady, 'tis impossible."

"No, it is very possible, Sally. Do you still wear that bonnet, the one with the wide brim and the little blue feather? Fetch it—and the brown dress you wear and your cloak."

"Oh, my lady!" cried Sally. "You can't mean to—"

"Quickly, Sally, fetch these things. And tell Amos and everyone you see that I am sending you on an errand."

"Oh, no, my lady." Sally was genuinely frightened.

"You have nothing to fear. You are only obeying my orders. Come, Sally, won't you do this for me?"

The young woman hesitated, for her devotion to Lady Georgina did not altogether undo her common sense. Yet her mistress had that stubborn look on her face, and Sally gave in, rushing off to do as Georgina requested.

She returned dressed in her cloak and bonnet and hiding her brown dress under the folds of the cloak. " 'Tis not what a lady should wear," protested Sally as Georgina took off her fashionable dress and slipped on her maid's well-worn frock.

"This will be fine." Georgina went to the door and called out, "And do hurry, Sally. If I am to stay here all day, I shall need these books from the lending library. I pray you hurry, and talk to no one along the way." She shut the door and smiled at her maid. "I shall remember your assistance, dear Sally, and I shall send for you soon." She pulled the cloak over her shoulders and adjusted the bonnet so it hid most of her face. Then, taking her reticule, which contained a few coins, she smiled once more at Sally and then hurried out.

The servant watching the back entrance of the house gave her only a passing glance, and she gave a sigh as she exited. Although her heart was pounding violently, Georgina walked slowly into the street and even nodded to the vigilant Perkins, who waved and called, "Good day, Sally."

She proceeded across the street and increased her pace as she got farther and farther from the house. She smiled at the ease with which she had eluded the earl's servants, but realized she could not relax until she had arrived at Penelope's house. Penelope would aid her, she had no doubt of that, and she vowed that never again would she spend a night under the roof of her heartless and unreasonable brother.

It was not far to Penelope's house, and Georgina hurried to the door. The butler could not contain his surprise at seeing Lady Georgina in such humble attire, but he said nothing and showed her in.

"I regret to say, my lady, that Miss Amesbury and Mrs. Grove have gone out."

"Out? Oh, dear, this is bad luck. Do you expect them back soon, Hemmings?"

"Not for several hours, my lady."

"Oh, dear. But I shall wait for them. And Hemmings . . ."

"Yes, my lady?"

"Do not tell anyone I am here. Please, Hemmings."

"As your ladyship wishes," said the butler, who, although reluctant to involve himself directly in any intrigues, was willing to do as Lady Georgina had requested.

Georgina made her way to the drawing room, where she sat nervously awaiting Penelope's return. Her cousin had left a book on the chair, and Georgina tried to read, but found concentration impossible. She stood up and began to pace the floor, wishing desperately that Penelope would return. After some twenty minutes of this nervous pacing, Georgina heard a commotion at the front door.

"Look here, I know Lady Georgina is here," said a voice she recognized as that of her brother's servant, Perkins. "Fetch her or we'll be obliged to search the house."

Georgina fled from the drawing room to the back door, and then outside and to the stables. A young groom was startled to see her, but recognized her immediately and made a respectful bow.

"Saddle a horse for me, please. Hurry!"

"But there are no horses here, my lady. Only that one o' yours, and she's no saddle horse."

Georgina looked around the stable and found that, indeed, her own poor Matilda was the only horse left there. "Then saddle her, please. Oh, do hurry!"

The urgency in her voice made protest impossible. The servant hastened to saddle the little mare, and then lifted Georgina up into the sidesaddle.

"Tell no one except Miss Amesbury, I pray you!" cried Georgina, and then she was off as fast as Matilda could carry her. The young groom stared after her with a combination of bewilderment and admiration, reflecting that highborn ladies were a very curious breed.

When Victor Ballanville awakened, it was nearly one o'clock. After leisurely sipping a cup of chocolate and spending a considerable amount of time discussing the day's attire with his valet, he left his room and joined his cousin Renwick. He had expected that Renwick, accustomed to the country, would have risen earlier, but he had not expected to find the marquis pacing about the drawing room like a caged tiger.

"I say, Hugh, what is the matter?"

Renwick stopped. "Oh Victor, so you are finally up. I found I could not sleep."

"My poor cousin," said Victor, yawning, "I suspect this unfortunate agitation results from those years of rising early. I also suspect that you have been thinking about Lady Georgina. She is a lady to cause many men to have sleepless nights."

"Don't be ridiculous."

"Oh, do you deny that you have been thinking about her?"

"Oh, very well, Victor. I have been thinking about her. Damned if I have done little else since I met her. She infuriates me! I could have cheerfully boxed her ears last night."

"My dear Sam Botts, don't be absurd. Admit that you are fond of the lady."

Renwick regarded his cousin in surprise. "Fond of her? By God, I dislike her heartily."

"Yes, yes, of course you do," returned Victor, with a knowing smile. "But don't you think it is time to confess to Penelope and Georgina that you are not Sam Botts? Why did you stop me last night?"

"I daresay the information would scarcely have pleased the lady. She was angry enough, it seemed to me."

Victor laughed. "I fear you are right."

The two cousins were interrupted by the appearance of Victor's butler, who announced the arrival of the Earl of Rumbridge. Before Victor could express his amazement at Rumbridge's visit, the Earl barged into the drawing room and stared belligerently at them.

"Ballanville," he said, "do you know where my sister has gone?"

"Lady Georgina? Heavens, Rumbridge! Is she missing? And if indeed she is, why would you think I should know anything about it?"

"You are in league with Penelope Amesbury."

"In league with her? I should hope so. We are to be married, after all."

"Did you go to Miss Amesbury's house?" asked Renwick. "Lady Georgina would surely have gone there."

Rumbridge regarded him with disapproval. "You, sir, must be Ballanville's cousin, the Marquis of Renwick."

Renwick nodded. "I am. But it seems to me, sir, that this is hardly the time for introductions. If you would find Lady Georgina, you had best inquire at Miss Amesbury's house."

"She was not there, and neither was Penelope. And when Penelope returned, she said she knew nothing about Georgina's whereabouts."

"I assure you I know nothing about it whatsoever," said Victor. "And do calm yourself, Rumbridge. You are undoubtedly upset over nothing."

"I warn you, Ballanville, I will not stand for your interference in my family affairs! If you know something, you had better tell me now!"

"And I warn you, sir, that I will not tolerate you barging into my house, acting like a madman and insulting me."

Rumbridge glared at them both and then turned to go. He paused at the door. "I caution you to say nothing about this to anyone. My sister's reputation is at stake."

"Do not fear that I will carry tales, Rumbridge."

The earl scowled. Saying nothing more, he hurried out.

"Now what do you make of that, Hugh? Most odd, I should say. Georgina, flown off? Oh, dear."

"Where might she have gone if not to Penelope's house?" said Renwick, who found the news quite unsettling.

"Dear me. I don't know. If she's not with Penelope . . . But I suspect my darling Penelope knows something about this. Let us dash over to see her."

The gentlemen arrived at Miss Amesbury's house and found Penelope quite upset. She explained that her butler had informed her that Georgina had been there, but had raced off when Rumbridge's men had arrived. "I have been waiting for word, but have heard nothing, and I am worried. The groom said that she rode off on Matilda, the horse that she and Sam rescued."

"Good God," said Victor. "That old nag? Then I daresay she could not have gone far."

"But where could she have gone?" asked Renwick.

"I'm sure I have no idea," replied Penelope. "But we must find her."

"Is there anyone else she might have turned to for help? Another relation, perhaps?"

"There are no other relations in town, Sam. But wait. Perhaps Rebecca Rosewood. She is a good friend; or perhaps Lady Darlington, but I really don't think so. And of course, there is Liddcott. But no, that is impossible."

"Who is this Liddcott?" said Renwick.

"Miss Liddcott, I should say. She was Georgina's governess, and she was very devoted to Georgina. But she is miles away in Huntley-on-Sea. No, Georgina would never go there. It is too far, perhaps thirty miles."

Victor nodded. "Not even Georgina would attempt such a journey by herself. It seems to me that we can do nothing but wait. Surely she will send word here."

"But Victor, perhaps I could inquire along the road to Huntley-on-Sea," suggested Renwick.

"That would not be a very good idea. I really doubt—"

"But you don't know what she would do, Vic. I may as well take a look."

"But you don't know the town."

"I know that road, I think. I could try, in any case, Victor. Miss Amesbury, do you have a horse I might borrow?"

"I suppose so, Sam, but I am sure there is no call for you to rush all over town."

"Please, Miss Amesbury."

"Oh, very well. Hemmings, show this gentleman to the stables and have Andrew saddle Beaumont."

Renwick hurried off, and Penelope turned suddenly to her fiancé. "I found Sam's reaction most odd. He is a strange fellow. He is—" Penelope stopped in midsentence. "He called you Victor, did he not? I am certain of it!"

"My dear," said Victor a trifle sheepishly. "I must explain something about Sam Botts."

12

IF GEORGINA SUTTONDALE HAD BEEN THINKing rationally, she would have dismissed the idea of riding to Huntley-on-Sea, a village some twenty-eight miles distant, as ridiculous. However, Georgina was too upset to be reasonable; and she had a sudden, overpowering urge to seek the counsel of her friend and mentor, Sophronia Liddcott.

She therefore guided Matilda through the maze of London streets and finally reached the outskirts of the city. There she asked directions of an obliging elderly gentleman and soon found herself riding along the road to Huntley-on-Sea. Lady Georgina gave little thought to the distance involved and the fact that such a journey could be hazardous for a lady traveling by herself. Instead, her thoughts were occupied by her brother Rumbridge's infamous behavior. With each step of the way, her resolve to escape from his control grew stronger.

Yet after riding some five miles southeast of town, her determination was somewhat shaken by the darkening sky and the deepening gloom of rain clouds. It was beginning to grow late, and Georgina had no idea what lay ahead. Rain began to fall, and she pulled her cloak tight around her. The rain soaked Sally's poor bonnet, and the blue feather that adorned it sagged pathetically.

Georgina patted Matilda's rain-soaked neck and urged her on. The road curved sharply to the left, and riding beyond the curve, Georgina spotted a building. As she approached, she recognized it as an inn by the battered sign that proclaimed the place "The Fighting Bear." Although this belligerent name was somewhat daunting, Georgina was relieved.

She was wet and tired and knew that darkness would soon force her to stop. She pulled Matilda up alongside The Fighting Bear, and a boy came out grudgingly to take the horse. She jumped down and, taking out her reticule, tossed him a coin. He looked sullenly at her and led Matilda off.

Georgina shrugged and walked to the entrance of the inn. A man exited the door and nearly bumped into her, causing her to drop her reticule into the mud. The man made profuse apologies and then picked up the tiny bag, which was ruined, and returned it to her.

It was a most inauspicious arrival, thought Georgina as she took her mud-covered reticule and entered The Fighting Bear. The inn was typical of many such places that dotted the roads throughout the kingdom. It was crowded with noisy people, and the smell of ale and boiled cabbage permeated the air. "Can I help you, miss?" said a portly middle-aged man, who Georgina took to be the innkeeper.

"I'd like supper and a room, if you please."

The innkeeper regarded her curiously. "Are you alone, then, miss?"

"Oh, I am expecting someone," said Georgina hastily.

"Your husband meeting you?"

"Yes, my husband."

Reassured that Georgina was a respectable married lady, the innkeeper directed her to a table near the fire. She took off her wet cloak, sat down, and warily regarded the other inhabitants. They were mostly men, although a few women could be seen, and most of the patrons were downing flagons of ale with great enthusiasm. Two young gentlemen seated near Georgina were engaged in a heated discussion about the merits of a particular race horse, and Georgina shivered with cold and turned toward the fire. Lonely and miserable, she reflected for the first time that perhaps she had acted too hastily.

The crowd grew noisier as the hour grew late, and Georgina thanked providence that everyone seemed to be ignoring her. A beleaguered tavern maid brought her a plate of boiled mutton and cabbage and a flagon of ale, and Georgina ate the meal slowly. She was too nervous to be very hungry, and the limp mutton was unappetizing. Still she finished it as best she could, eager to leave the public room for the safety of whatever lodging the inn could provide.

"That will be sixpence if you please," said the tavern maid, coming to take Georgina's plate.

She fumbled with her reticule and was horrified to find it empty. Her coins were gone. "Oh, dear, I don't know what happened." She thought suddenly of the man who had picked up her bag outside the inn. "I fear I've been robbed."

"Lord, miss," said the maid. "I've got to have the money."

"But you see, I have been robbed. I haven't any money."

The maid shook her head and left, and soon returned with the innkeeper. "Daisy said you've been robbed."

"Indeed I have."

The innkeeper regarded her with suspicion. "I must say, miss, it ain't usual to have women coming here unescorted. I don't like it much. And it seems you have been most conveniently robbed."

Georgina was outraged. "You think I am lying to you!"

"I won't say that, but I know females of your kind. Seen them before. Look respectable and even talk like a lady, but out to cheat me out of a meal."

"Indeed, sir, if that is the usual caliber of your meals, I cannot understand why anyone should want to cheat you of one." Georgina immediately regretted these words, for the innkeeper looked very angry.

"Do not worry about the payment, for my husband shall soon be here."

"Your husband, eh? If this husband o' yours was coming, he'd o' been here by now. I think you've been telling tales."

"You have no right to talk to me in such a manner."

"Oh don't I? My, ain't you a fine lady. Well, I shall call the constable and you may tell him your tale."

"Oh, wait!" Georgina was horrified at the thought. "Can't you give me some time? I swear I shall pay you."

"Now you're being polite. I like that much better. Very well, I'll not call the constable. Instead, I'll give you the opportunity to settle your account in other ways."

Georgina tried not to look shocked. "What do you mean?"

"My Daisy is near exhausted, and we've a large crowd. If you'll assist Daisy with the ale and the dishes, I'll forget your debt."

"You want me to be a barmaid?" Georgina was so astounded she could barely speak.

"You don't fool me by that fancy talk. You and Daisy has much in common, I don't doubt."

The insolence of the man was almost more than Georgina could bear, and the idea of serving ale to a roomful of drunken and near-drunken louts was hardly appealing. Still, there seemed little choice. Georgina nodded her assent.

She soon found herself in an apron and cap, bringing mugs of ale to the customers, and the absurdity of the situation was not lost upon her. She wondered what the Prince Regent would say if he knew, or Rumbridge. The horrifying thought that someone she knew might see her there crossed her mind, but she instantly dismissed it. Certainly The Fighting Bear was not frequented by members of the *haut ton*.

It did not take Georgina long to develop a great deal of respect for barmaids. The work was hard, but what was worse was the abuse that accompanied it. The men patted and pinched her and made lewd remarks, and at her shocked expression they laughed and made indecent proposals. It was difficult to restrain herself from dousing the offenders with ale, but she knew the innkeeper would not take kindly to such treatment of his customers.

Into this rowdy scene came three soldiers dressed in red uniforms and eager for ale. Georgina brought it, keeping her eyes downcast and hoping to avoid their comments and roving hands. "My, she's a pretty wench," said one of the soldiers.

"Aye, sergeant," said one of the others, casting an appraising eye over her.

"Come here, my dear."

"I've work to do, sir," said Georgina, walking away.

The sergeant reached out quickly and grabbed her by the wrist. "Come here, I say." He pulled her roughly and she fell into his lap, whereupon he threw a burly arm around her and kissed her roughly on the lips. The other two men cheered him loudly.

Georgina pulled away furiously and slapped him hard across the face. The sergeant blinked, startled at the force of the blow. He shook his head and then grinned at her. "Full of fight, are you? I like that." He pulled her toward him again, and she struggled to escape.

"How dare you, you oaf!" cried Georgina, and the other soldiers laughed loudly as the sergeant planted another kiss on Georgina's lips and with one hand caressed her breast. Summoning all her strength, Georgina tried to extricate herself from the man's grip, but he held her fast and laughed at her struggles. "Let go of me, you vile pig!" she cried, tears of frustration coming to her face.

"Let her go." A stern masculine voice startled the sergeant, who looked up to see a well-dressed gentleman staring down at him with murderous rage. Georgina gasped as she beheld Renwick, his face dark with anger and his blue eyes gleaming with fury.

"I said let go of the lady."

Georgina took advantage of the sergeant's surprise to pull away from him and jump up.

"Oh, Sam!" she cried.

He pulled her behind him, and with a lightning-fast movement grasped the sergeant by the front of his uniform and pulled him to his feet. "Who are you?" cried the soldier, but before he could complete the question, Renwick directed a blow to his stomach and the man doubled over, gasping for breath.

The marquis turned defiantly to the other two soldiers. "Do I have to fight you, too?"

The soldiers hesitated; then one rushed to aid the sergeant. The other stared at Renwick. He had no wish to get into the fray, since he saw that Renwick appeared to be one of the nobs and it was foolhardy to tangle with angry aristocrats—especially ones who could punch as well as any pugilist he had ever seen.

"No call for anger, guv'nor," said the soldier. "The sergeant was just having a bit o' fun."

Renwick did not deign to reply, but directed a scornful look at the three soldiers and then pulled Georgina away. "My God, what are you about? You're dressed like a tavern wench!"

"Oh, Sam!" Georgina felt suddenly very weak and, to Renwick's great embarrassment, burst into sobs and threw herself into his arms.

Renwick, rather alarmed at finding Lady Georgina in his arms, comforted her as best he could and then led her to the far side of the room. The events had created much interest, and all eyes were upon them. "Mind your business, now," shouted Renwick, and the others looked quickly away and whispered to each other.

The innkeeper, worried at seeing the expensive cut of Renwick's clothes, was suddenly very solicitous. "Oh, I'm so sorry, sir. I can explain everything."

"Can you?" said Renwick, looking every inch the noble lord, and Georgina reflected that Sam Botts could be a most formidable man.

"There was a misunderstanding, sir. Your wife had no money, and you had not arrived, and—"

Georgina had by now sufficiently recovered to glare at the innkeeper. "There is no excuse for your behavior. Did I not tell you that my husband was arriving?"

"Yes, yes; you're right about that, ma'am. I do hope you and your husband will find it in your hearts to forgive me."

Renwick had thought the references to himself as Georgina's husband rather odd, but since Georgina was for some reason perpetuating this misconception, he said nothing.

"I shall make amends," continued the innkeeper. "Do follow me, please."

Georgina and Renwick exchanged glances and then followed the innkeeper from the public room and up a narrow staircase to one of the guest rooms. "My best room, this is," he said, opening the door.

"Is it?" asked Georgina, peering into the small, dingy room.

"Yes, ma'am, and I hope you and your husband will be my guests. I shall send supper up to you."

"Is this the only room you have?" said Georgina, eyeing it with distaste.

"You've seen how crowded we are, ma'am. 'Tis my only room and my best." The innkeeper handed Renwick a candle and retreated hurriedly.

"Oh, my," said Georgina, looking from the dingy room to Renwick. "What are we to do now, Sam?"

"First, my lady, I think some explanations are in order."

"Oh, Sam, it was dreadful." They entered the room, and Georgina sat down upon the bed while Renwick pulled up a rickety old chair, the only other piece of furniture in the room.

"I was robbed, and the innkeeper took me for some sort of dishonest woman and threatened to call the constable if I did not assist his maid Daisy."

"So he had you work like a common tavern wench? Damn him! I shall make him rue his poor judgment."

The vehemence of this speech surprised Georgina. "Do not be so angry at the man. I admit I did look suspicious coming in alone, and I told him I was meeting my husband here."

"Which is why he took me to be your tardy husband."

"Yes." Georgina smiled for the first time. "Poor Sam, I'm sorry I thrust that role upon you."

Renwick, smiling in return, realized with a start that he could wish for nothing more at that moment than to be Lady Georgina's husband. Indeed, he was nearly overcome by an urge to take that lady into his arms again. Realizing that under the circumstances such thoughts were quite dangerous, Renwick turned his mind to other matters.

"Your brother was dashing about town trying to find you. I fear, my lady, that the earl is very upset."

"My brother Rumbridge is always upset about something. But, Sam, how did you find me?"

"It was not so difficult. After Miss Amesbury told me about your Miss Liddcott, I thought you might try to go to see her. I found that this is the only road to take. And since Matilda is a most distinctive horse and it is not common for ladies to ride unescorted through the countryside, a number of persons remembered seeing you pass."

"It seems that I detect some disapproval in your tone, Sam."

"I do indeed disapprove, my lady. I think it foolish and dangerous for you to fly off as you did." He expected her to become angry at his words, but she only nodded.

"You are right, Sam. I was stupid."

He regarded her in some surprise. "You are strangely agreeable tonight, Lady Georgina."

She laughed. "I think it is because I am so exhausted. I feel as though I could sleep forever." She patted the bed. "Even in this decrepit old thing. Oh, dear."

"My lady?"

"This is an awkward situation, is it not?"

"And why is that?" Renwick grinned.

"You are terrible!" cried Georgina.

Renwick laughed. "You go to bed, my lady. I shall go down and obtain my supper from that innkeeper."

"But where will you sleep?"

"Don't worry about me. I shall manage. Good night."

"Good night, Sam. And thank you for rescuing me."

He smiled, and it was now Georgina who experienced a dangerous urge to throw her arms around his broad shoulders.

"My, ain't we getting on well?" he said in mock astonishment. "Good night, my lady." He smiled again and was gone.

Renwick spent a restless night in the public room after he finally fell asleep at the table. The innkeeper found it very odd that a gentleman having a wife like his waiting for him would be so reluctant to go to his room. However, he did not make any comments, but went to bed himself, leaving Renwick asleep at the table, his head resting upon his arms.

As dawn's faint light permeated the room, Renwick awakened. Stiff, he got up from the table and stretched. The room was empty except for an elderly man, who was snoring peacefully in his chair. Renwick walked over to the window and peered out, noting that the sky was clear and there was no sign of more rain.

He turned away from the window and thought of Georgina. She was without a doubt the most exasperating female he had ever met. Well, he decided, it was time to awaken that exasperating female and return to town. He crept up the stairs and knocked lightly at the door of her room. "Lady Georgina," he whispered.

"Sam, is that you?" came a voice from behind the door.

"Of course."

"Wait just a moment."

Renwick stood there, his arms folded in front of him, and a short time later, Georgina opened the door. Clad in her maid's plain dress, her hair uncombed and tangled from sleep, Georgina reflected that she must look a sight. The marquis, however, thought she looked lovely; but he was in no mood to tell her so.

"Are you ready now?"

"Yes, Sam." She looked at his unshaven face and rumpled clothes. "Oh, dear, it looks as though you didn't sleep at all."

"I slept very little, as a matter of fact, but that does not signify. If you are ready, m'lady, I think we had best be off."

"Be off? And where are we going, Sam?"

"Why, back to London, of course."

"You may be going back to town, but I assure you I am not." She glanced back into the room. "Oh, I have forgotten Sally's hat." She stepped back into the room and took up the hat, then walked back out the door, passing by Renwick and starting down the stairs.

The marquis frowned and followed her downstairs, where they were met by the innkeeper. Georgina directed a haughty gaze at the man, and Renwick scowled at him. Daunted by such a greeting, the innkeeper bade them good morning. Renwick scowled again, but tossed a silver coin to the man, who seemed quite relieved to get it.

"What do you mean, you'll not go back to town?" said Renwick as they stepped outside.

"I mean just that. I concede it is foolhardy of me, but I have gone this far and I shall continue on to Huntley-on-Sea."

"Continue on? By God, that's the most ridiculous thing I ever heard in my life."

"Is it? It is not so very far, and the weather is good." Georgina walked over to the stables, and Renwick followed.

"You have no money."

"I need none. I shall arrive at Liddy's house by early afternoon. Oh, Matilda, there you are, my girl. I hope you are well rested."

Matilda looked expectantly at her mistress.

"You can't be serious."

Georgina turned her brown eyes upon Renwick, and

they had their usual disconcerting effect upon that gentleman. "Look, Sam, I'm very grateful to you about last night. But I'm not going back. My life with my brother has become unendurable."

"But you could go to Miss Amesbury."

"I doubt whether I could go to her. I am certain my brother has employed his villains to watch her house. Oh, where is that stable boy?"

The sullen youth was nowhere to be seen, and Georgina shrugged and took up Matilda's bridle. "I shall have to saddle her myself, it seems."

"Oh, I'll do it," said Renwick, taking the bridle from her and slipping the bit into Matilda's mouth. "You are the most stubborn female," he muttered as he saddled the little mare. Georgina smiled.

"Thank you very much, Sam. Will you help me up?"

"As soon as my horse is ready." He led his own horse from the stable and began to saddle it.

"You're leaving now, too, Sam? I hope you will tell Mr. Ballanville that I am fine. No, wait. Don't tell him or Miss Amesbury that you have seen me. Please, Sam."

Renwick threw his saddle up onto the horse's back. "I'll not be telling them anything."

"Thank you, Sam."

"Oh, don't be so quick to thank me. Were I going to London, I'd tell them first thing."

"What do you mean?"

"I mean, Lady Georgina, that I am escorting you to Huntley-on-Sea."

"Oh, Sam! Would you?"

"I can't let you go off alone, can I?"

"But what will Mr. Ballanville say?"

"He'll say I'm a fool," said Renwick, turning to her and lifting her easily up onto Matilda's back. "And he'll be right."

Renwick then mounted his own horse and avoided Georgina's quizzical gaze.

It proved to be a perfect day for a ride in the country, and Georgina soon found that she was enjoying herself despite Renwick's bad-tempered avoidance of conversation and the knowledge that she must look terrible. Matilda was not the sort of horse her ladyship was accustomed to, but neither was the little mare the decrepit cart horse one might suppose her to be.

They traveled for a time in silence, and Georgina viewed Renwick's stern expression with amusement. "Are you in pain, Sam?" she said, smiling. "How grim you look."

"You cannot expect me to be overjoyed at being part of this foolish scheme of yours."

Georgina was suddenly irritated. "I did not ask you to come with me. I should prefer you leave now if you are going to ride all the way in silence and stare at me as if I were some sort of criminal."

"Well, Lady Georgina, running off like this scarcely does credit to your reputation."

"My reputation. How dare you, Sam Botts? You are not one to talk of reputations. You who cavort about town like a notorious rake."

Renwick pulled his horse up short and stared at her in indignation. "Cavort, you say?"

"Yes, cavort. I could call it worse, but I am a lady. I refer, of course, to your conduct with Fanny Terrell and Emily Carlyle."

"That again? By God, you seem to be preoccupied with that subject. Of what concern is it to you?"

"None," snapped Georgina, flicking her riding crop at Matilda's hindquarters, and leaving Renwick behind.

The marquis frowned and hurried after her. After this unfortunate exchange of words, there were no more attempts at conversation. They both continued glumly along the road, until Georgina spied a man standing at the side of the road beside a cart. He waved at them as they approached, and Georgina saw that his rough cart was disabled. A wheel lay beside it on the road, and the cart tipped precariously to one side.

"Having trouble?" said Renwick.

"Aye, sir. Hit that rock there and the wheel come off. Would appreciate some help, sir."

Renwick got off his horse and surveyed the cart wheel. "Doesn't appear damaged. I'll help you get it on again." He tied his horse's rein to the cart and then turned to help Georgina down from Matilda. Georgina appeared none too enthusiastic about accepting his aid, but permitted the marquis to lift her down.

The cart owner lifted his worn hat in greeting. "Good day to you, ma'am."

"Good day, sir."

"Always having trouble with the old cart," explained the man, a middle-aged fellow with greying hair, merry eyes, and a face tanned and wrinkled by many years in the sun.

"It's not too serious," said Renwick. "I'll lift it up, and you put the wheel on."

"It's heavy, sir," warned the man, but Renwick only shrugged.

"Take the wheel and be ready." The marquis then crouched and, grasping the aged cart, lifted it with apparent ease. Renwick was proud of his great strength and not averse to demonstrating it. The cart owner quickly lifted the wheel into place on the axle.

"There, that should do it," said Renwick.

"Aye, thankee, sir. My, you're a strong gentleman."

Georgina smiled at this remark. "Do be careful, Sam," she said, trying to sound unimpressed. "You must not strain your back." He only frowned at her.

"Good as new," said the cart owner. "Good as new. I can not thank you enough, sir."

Renwick, who had rarely gone all morning without a hearty breakfast, had noted that the contents of the cart included two round cheeses and a loaf of bread. "If you would want to thank me, sir, you'll allow me to buy a bit of cheese and bread from you. This lady and I are very hungry."

"Hungry, you say? Why, sir, you're welcome to all I have, but if you please, I'd be right honored if you and your lady would come home with me for a bit o' lunch. My wife would be proud to have you."

"You are kind, but we could not impose upon you and your wife," began Georgina, who, like Renwick, was growing very hungry.

" 'Twould be no trouble, and the least I could do to thank you. And though the fare won't be fancy, 'twill be some better than a mere slice o' cheese. My house is just up the road not half a mile. I insist upon it."

The idea of lunch was irresistible to the marquis. "If you are certain we would cause you no trouble, Mr. . . ."

"Parker. Jack Parker is my name, sir." Renwick extended his hand, which Mr. Parker shook vigorously. Parker then looked expectantly at the marquis and Georgina.

Realizing an introduction was in order, Georgina said hesitantly, "Oh, I am . . . Mrs. Botts, and this is my husband, Sam."

"Very glad am I to make your acquaintance. You are fine folks, and 'tis lucky for me you happened by. But we'd best get on to the house before it gets any later."

Mr. Parker climbed into his cart and picked up his reins. "Just ahead is the house," he said, flicking the reins. "Just follow me."

The little cart started off down the road, and Renwick turned to Georgina. "So you're still Mrs. Botts, my lady?"

Georgina frowned. "What else could I say? But don't imagine I enjoy this charade."

Renwick grinned. "Not for a moment, ma'am. But we'd best be getting along. I am devilish hungry. Come on, then. Allow me to help you up."

Renwick's strong hands encircled her waist, and he lifted her neatly into the saddle. Georgina didn't wait for him to mount, but hurried after the cart. Renwick watched her for a moment, then shrugged, mounted his own horse, and followed after the exasperating Lady Georgina.

13

MR. PARKER'S HOUSE WAS A VERY MODEST dwelling, but it was not without charm, perched as it was on the green hillside and shaded with numerous trees. Georgina found it quaint and picturesque, and for a moment almost envied Mr. Parker, whose simple agrarian life she imagined was as carefree as it was dull.

Renwick said nothing as he helped her down from her horse, and they were ushered inside the cottage by Mr. Parker. "We have guests, Meg."

"Guests?" Mrs. Parker appeared undaunted by the arrival of unexpected guests. She was a tall, sturdy, grey-haired woman of calm disposition, who now wiped her hands on her apron and advanced to meet the newcomers.

" 'Tis Mr. and Mrs. Botts. I met them on the road. Mr. Botts helped me with the wheel on the cart. It came off again, Meg."

"How do you do, Mrs. Parker?" said Georgina, smiling graciously. "Do forgive this intrusion."

"Intrusion?" said Mrs. Parker, studying Georgina and Renwick curiously. " 'Tis good to have company, especially folks that help my husband. And you've come at the right time. The stew is ready and there is plenty for all of us."

"Very kind of you, Mrs. Parker," said Renwick.

"Then sit down, both of you." Mrs. Parker pointed to the table. "I'll fetch the plates."

Renwick and Georgina obediently sat down and were soon supplied with plates of hearty and palatable stew.

"This is delicious, Mrs. Parker," said Georgina.

" 'Tis Meg's special stew," said Parker, joining them

while his wife poured glasses of ale and set them before her guests and husband. Finally, Mrs. Parker sat down too.

" 'Tis not much," she said modestly.

"It is excellent," said the marquis, devouring the stew with a relish that pleased his hosts immensely.

"So you folks are passing by, then?"

"Yes, Mrs. Parker," said Georgina. "We are on our way to Huntley-on-Sea."

"Then you've not far to go." Mrs. Parker passed a basket of bread to Georgina. "Come far, have you?"

"Not very far," replied Georgina noncommittally.

"When I first saw them, I reckoned they was gentlefolk visiting the squire," commented Mr. Parker. "You're not guests of the squire, are you?"

"The squire?" said Renwick, taking a drink of ale. "No, indeed."

Georgina thought she detected relief on Mrs. Parker's face. "Who is this squire, Mrs. Parker?"

"Squire Robert Allenby. He owns all the lands hereabouts."

"Allenby," said Georgina, trying to place that gentleman. "No, I don't think I have ever heard the name."

"Never heard of Squire Allenby? Would to God I could say that," said Mrs. Parker.

"Meg!" Mr. Parker gave his wife a warning look and abruptly changed the subject. "You interested in hogs, Mr. Botts?"

"Hogs?" repeated Renwick, and Georgina nearly burst into laughter at his expression. "Why, yes, I am."

"Are you a farmer, then, Mr. Botts?"

"Well, not exactly, but I do have an interest in farming, Mr. Parker."

"Glad to hear it. I've been a farmer on this land all my life, and we've done well enough, eh, mother?"

Mrs. Parker nodded.

"Raised up six children here. All growed, they are, with families o' their own. They all live hereabouts—all except Harry, who's off to America. But I'd like you to see my sow, Mr. Botts. She's a dear one, and none better in the shire."

To Georgina's considerable surprise, Renwick acted quite eager to see Mr. Parker's sow, and after finishing

ROGUE'S MASQUERADE 143

their lunch, the two men left the table. Georgina had declined a belated invitation to accompany them and assisted Mrs. Potter with cleaning up.

As she carried plates from the table, it struck Lady Georgina that she had never before performed such domestic services. She hoped that she would not appear too awkward, but Mrs. Parker was too intent upon the work at hand to notice that Georgina seemed ill-at-ease with kitchen chores.

"We are very grateful for lunch, Mrs. Parker," said Georgina, wiping a dish with a cloth Mrs. Parker had handed her.

"You're welcome to it, Mrs. Botts. Good to have company. Now that my youngest girl's married, I miss having a woman in the house to talk to. 'Course I see my girl Hattie all the time. See all of my children regular, but for Harry. He went off to America and lives in Massachusetts. 'Tis a strange name, Massachusetts. By my way o' thinking, a place with such a name should be wild and savage. But not so, says Harry." Mrs. Parker put her last dish into the cupboard, then reached into a pocket in her apron. "Here's a letter come from Harry all the way from America. He's only been there one year and already owns his own blacksmith shop. America is a land of opportunity. Harry says a man's birth don't matter much there and he can be a great man if he works hard. He was always a hard-working lad, my Harry."

"You must miss him."

Mrs. Parker nodded and put the letter back into her pocket. "Aye, but he's doing well and says America is a fine place. But I won't go on about it. You and your man are probably in a hurry to be off. When my husband starts on about that sow of his, it's nigh on impossible to stop him."

Georgina followed Mrs. Parker from the house and—across the yard to where Renwick and Mr. Parker stood leaning against the fence and talking intently.

Georgina's interest in livestock was confined to horses, but it was with fascination that she beheld Mr. Parker's prize sow. The enormous black creature stood regarding Mr. Parker with doglike affection.

"Beautiful animal, is she not, Mrs. Botts?" said Renwick, smiling mischievously at Georgina.

"Yes, indeed," said Georgina, whose sense of the aesthetically beautiful did not include pigs. "A most impressive animal. But Mr. Botts, do you not think that we should be going?"

Renwick nodded. "I was just about to take a look at Mr. Parker's cow. She's been doing poorly, it seems."

"I'd be grateful if you'd take a look."

Georgina stared quizzically at Renwick and wondered if he had any knowledge of animal husbandry, or if he was posing as a farmer just as he had learned to pose as a gentleman.

"Jack Parker," admonished Mrs. Parker. "Don't take all of Mr. Botts's time. He should be off."

"Don't worry. We have enough time for a quick look."

Mrs. Parker directed an apologetic look at Georgina, who assured her it was all right. The men started toward the small barn, but the sound of hoofbeats caused everyone to stop and look toward the road. A rider was aproaching them on a bay horse. "The squire!" said Mrs. Parker, a look of distress on her face. "Jack! The squire!"

Mr. Parker muttered something, and Renwick directed his gaze toward the approaching rider. He was a well-dressed young man of slight build who handled his horse with consummate skill. He turned the animal into the Parkers' yard and pulled up his horse.

"Parker; Meg."

"Squire." Mr. Parker pulled at his forelock in a respectful gesture.

The horseman looked from the Parkers to Renwick, and then his eye fell upon Georgina. He studied her appreciatively, his eye roaming from her face to her toes and back again with unabashed insolence. Georgina met this scrutiny with an indignant look, and Renwick scowled.

"You have company, it seems, Parker."

"Aye, sir. Mr. Botts and his wife were passing by, and Mr. Botts give me a hand with the wagon."

"How very kind of you, sir," said the squire, with a condescending smile that irritated Renwick. He eyed the marquis, noting the cut of the fashionable coat that marked him as a gentleman of means. "Botts, you say? Well, Mr. Botts, I am Squire Allenby, and I am grateful to anyone who helps one of my people." He smiled again and then dismounted, handing his reins to Mrs. Parker as if she were a stable boy. Georgina thought this very rude and looked disapprovingly at the young man, who, oblivious of her unspoken rebuke, continued talking to Renwick. "I expect that old Jack has been showing you that sow of his. He's so very proud of it. Pity you'll not have her much longer, Parker."

"But, squire . . ." began Parker, but Allenby cut him off with a gesture.

"I have little time, Parker. Frazer tells me you've not paid all of your rent."

"After the harvest, sir, you'll get all what's owed you. Please, squire, you can see the crop is a good one."

"I can see only a tenant who has paid me nothing in a year. I'm sending a man to take that sow of yours and whatever else there is of value." Squire Allenby looked haughtily at Parker's cottage. "I daresay there isn't much."

Allenby's manners were causing Renwick's Ballanville temper to come to the fore. "You can't mean to take the man's sow."

Allenby smiled. "Indeed I do, sir, and if you were not a stranger here, you would understand why. This man has failed to pay the rent due me. As a gentleman, sir, you must be aware of the rights of a landlord such as myself."

"I know well of such rights," said Renwick, "but it seems you cannot recognize a good tenant. Mr. Parker's crops are excellent, and although I am only recently acquainted with him, it seems he is a hard-working man. The condition of this property attests to that. I should think myself fortunate to have him as a tenant on my estates." Georgina regarded Renwick with some surprise, noting his mention of "my estates" and wondering if his two-week pose as a noble lord had clouded reality. He looked every inch the proud nobleman, and Georgina was worried that he would forget his place entirely.

"Please, Sam," she said. "Guard your temper."

"Good advice," said Allenby, who resented Renwick's words. It was not often that anyone dared to disagree with him, and he was irritated that the well-dressed stranger would take his tenant's part. "It appears you are sensible as well as lovely, madam. Pray, remind your husband that he would do well to mind his own business. I do not appreciate his interference and I do not like strangers informing me of the merits of my tenants."

"And I do not like your tone, sir." Renwick's eyes flashed ominously, and he took a step toward the squire.

Georgina, frightened by Renwick's expression, placed a restraining hand on his arm. "Please, Sam!"

Renwick stopped, but glared menacingly at Allenby, who was rather daunted by Renwick's belligerence. The marquis was much taller than he and outweighed him by fifty pounds, and the squire was not so foolhardy as to risk coming to blows.

"I will remain here no longer," he said, quickly taking his reins from Mrs. Parker and leaping agilely into the saddle. "I will not be bullied, sir." He directed a contemptuous look at Renwick and then turned to Parker. "You have tried my patience once too often, Parker. You will pack your things and remove yourself from my property within two days. I shall send the constable to see to it that you do so."

"But, squire, your father told me—"

"Dammit, Parker! I don't give a hang about my father's promises. It seems you forget that I am squire now." He pointed his riding crop threateningly at Parker. 'I am sick to death of you and all of your kind, blaming me for your own sloth and stupidity and getting strangers to bully me. No, Parker, you would have been better served if your friend had kept quiet. Remember, you have two days to be gone. And my man will come for *my* sow." Allenby turned his horse sharply and galloped away.

"Oh, Jack." Mrs. Parker, horror-stricken, stared after the squire. "He cannot mean it."

Mr. Parker nodded. "I fear he does, Meg."

"Damn the man!" muttered Renwick. "I should have beat some sense into him."

"Sam Botts!" Georgina turned angrily to Renwick. "Haven't you done enough? It is you who have provoked this squire to evict the Parkers."

"No, Mrs. Botts," interrupted Jack Parker. " 'Tis no fault of Mr. Botts. 'Twas only a matter of time before he'd have forced us out."

Renwick looked chagrined. "No, my . . . wife is right. I did lose my temper. And I fear you are both the worse for it."

"Indeed so," said Georgina. "If only you could have kept silent."

"How could you expect me to say nothing when a man like that speaks to me in such a manner?"

"He is a man of property and a gentleman, and you are Sam Botts. It seems you have forgotten that."

"And so I have," said Renwick testily. "And I expect, if I had kept silent, you could have charmed Allenby into reason."

"I daresay I could not have done worse than you, sir. It was obvious that harsh words and bluster would do no good. And it is the Parkers who will suffer for your rashness."

Renwick frowned at Georgina and turned to Parker. "I am sorry, Mr. Parker. There must be something I can do. I shall go to see Allenby and reason with him."

"Indeed not, Sam!" Georgina shook her head. "You would only make matters worse."

"Aye, sir, Mrs. Botts is right. But don't fret, Mr. Botts. 'Tis not your fault. Master Robert has wanted me gone ever since his father died. There's naught that can be done."

"But what will you do?" asked Georgina.

Mrs. Parker shook her head. "I reckon we'll go to my daughter Mary at Litchfield. She'll make room for us. A dutiful girl, is Mary. Don't you worry about us. 'Tis our problem, after all. And you folks should be going if you wish to reach Huntley-on-Sea early. My husband and myself will be fine."

"This is the most damnable business," muttered Renwick. He paused. "But what of your cow? I might at least take a look at her before we go." He looked at Georgina. "If my wife does not object too much."

"I do not object in the least, Mr. Botts. By all means assist Mr. Parker. Perhaps you can make amends for some of the damage you have done."

"It would be kind of you to see her," replied Parker, trying to put a stop to the young couple's squabbling. "The cow's back this way, sir."

Renwick and Parker retreated to the barn, and Georgina and Mrs. Parker returned to the house. "I have lived in this house all my married life, Mrs. Botts, since I was eighteen. 'Twill be hard to leave it."

"But why is this Squire Allenby so intent on having you go?"

"The squire? Master Robert has no love for anyone. I've known him since he were only a babe, and never have I heard a kind word said of him. He took a particular dislike to my man and my son Harry. Never did know why, but 'twas Master Robert who caused my Harry to be off to America. The old squire was a good man and a fair one, but no father and son were ever more different. But 'tis no use to go on about Master Robert. He is the squire, and folk like us can do naught. 'Tis his land and we cannot pay the rent."

Mrs. Parker's gloomy thoughts were interrupted by the sound of someone at the door. She pulled it open and faced a stout man in well-worn work clothes. "Will Martin. This *is* a day for visitors. Jack is in the barn, Will." He nodded and left without a word. "Will's our neighbor, and a good friend to us. He's married to my cousin Nan. Will Martin is not a man to waste words on womenfolk, but he'll talk for hours to my man about his animals. I reckon your husband could be some time getting away from the two of them. Will you have tea?"

Georgina shook her head. "No thank you, Mrs. Parker." She wondered at the older woman's calmness in light of Squire Allenby's visit, and realized suddenly that the Parkers' troubles had made her forget her own. She remembered her brother Rumbridge, and reflected that a man like Robert Allenby made Rumbridge look very likable in comparison. She knitted her brows in concentration. Perhaps if she had tried to talk to Allenby, he might have been persuaded to give the Parkers time to pay the rent. After all, she had once so charmed a very difficult Prussian ambassador that the Prince Regent had exclaimed that she should be in the diplomatic corps. Of course, thought Georgina, not everyone was susceptible to her charm; Sam Botts was proof of that.

The cottage door was opened, and Mr. Parker put his head in. "Will's having trouble with his sheep. Mr. Botts and me are going to take a look."

"But Mr. Botts cannot waste his time—" began Mrs. Parker.

"It's perfectly all right," said Renwick's voice. "We'll be back soon."

"Soon, is it?" Mrs. Parker shook her head. "Not the way Will Martin can talk. Oh, dear."

"It's quite all right, Mrs. Parker," said Georgina.

Mrs. Parker looked skeptical. "Mind you, Jack, don't keep Mr. Botts too long!" She turned to Georgina. "Men! They've no sense. I fear you'll have a long wait."

"I don't mind, I assure you." Georgina looked thoughtful for a moment. "Does the squire have any family? Anyone who would listen to reason?"

"No. His parents are dead, God rest their souls. His younger brother Maxwell is in the navy, and his sister Catherine lives in Scotland. There's no one to say no to him—but then there never was, except the old squire."

"Mrs. Parker, would you mind if I took a ride? I need a bit of air. That frightful man distressed me, and I could do with a bit of exercise."

"Not at all," replied Mrs. Parker in some surprise, "but I thought you'd been riding all morning."

"Oh, I know it seems odd. I shall be back shortly." Georgina started toward the door. "Oh, Mrs. Parker, which way is it to the squire's house? I want to be sure that I avoid him. I never want to see that man again."

Mrs. Parker nodded and gave Georgina the directions to the squire's house. After assuring her hostess she would avoid the place, Georgina left the house and in a short while was perched upon Matilda and heading direct for Allenby Hall.

14

ALLENBY HALL WAS A GREY STONE BUILDing with none of the charm of so many English country houses. It was a grim, formless structure that would have caused anyone convinced of the superiority of English architects to reconsider.

Lady Georgina approached this bleak edifice of weathered stone and was suddenly beset with misgivings. Surely she was mad to think, even for a moment, that she could persuade Squire Allenby to adopt a more lenient posture toward the Parkers. She was a fool to interfere, she told herself. Yet Georgina was not one to be easily deterred, and she urged Matilda on.

A footman in soiled livery met her at the door and took Matilda's head. Mustering all her dignity, Georgina dismounted. She ignored the footman, who was eyeing her strangely, and walked to the door, which was opened by a butler. "I am here to see Squire Allenby," she said in a manner befitting the daughter of an earl.

The butler looked about to see who had accompanied this aristocratic though shabbily dressed young lady. "I am alone. You may announce Lady . . . that is to say, announce Mrs. Botts, if you please."

The butler grudgingly led her to a drawing room, which contained heavy, old-fashioned furniture that looked as though it could withstand the onslaught of artillery fire. Georgina surveyed the room with distaste, noting the numerous animal-head trophies that adorned the wall and gave the room a barbaric, medieval appearance.

"Mrs. Botts, is it? By God, I am surprised, but maybe I shouldn't be. Indeed, I wasn't sure what to make of you."

ROGUE'S MASQUERADE 151

Georgina turned around to face Robert Allenby. "I knew immediately what to make of you, sir," she replied.

Allenby laughed and, without saying another word, threw himself into one of the chairs. Georgina, who was unused to gentlemen who would sit while leaving a lady standing, disregarded his lack of manners.

"I have come, sir, because I was worried that my . . . husband's words have prejudiced you against the Parkers."

"And what are the Parkers to you?"

"Why, nothing. We are barely acquainted, but I should not like to see them ill-treated on our account. I know you were offended by my husband's words, but he is in no way connected with Mr. Parker. I hoped that I might persuade you to reconsider the matter. Perhaps you could allow them to stay until the harvest, when they could pay you."

"Perhaps I could," said Allenby, "but I doubt I will. I do not like the Parkers, nor any of their sort. You, though . . ." The squire grinned at her. "You I like very well indeed."

Georgina tried to overlook Allenby's insolent manner and leering grin. "How much do the Parkers owe you, sir, for you to treat them in such a manner?"

"I don't see how it is any concern of yours, madam, but I don't mind telling you. Forty pounds."

"Is that all? I can scarcely believe you would evict them for such a small sum."

"You amaze me, Mrs. Botts. From your dress I would think forty pounds would seem a goodly sum. And yet from your manner and the way your so-called husband was dressed, perhaps you are no stranger to even larger sums."

"My 'so-called' husband? How dare you, sir!"

"My dear lady, I pride myself that I am an observant man. I saw how you are dressed and how that husband of yours dressed, and then I saw two horses, one very fine and one quite fit for nothing but food for dogs. And my man tells me you have ridden on this extraordinary creature. What self-respecting man would allow his wife to ride an animal like that?"

"You are quite mistaken. I prefer that horse."

"As you prefer going without a wedding ring?" Georgina looked down at her hand. "You are no 'Mrs.' Botts, my dear. You are his mistress, and I wager he is a lucky man. But look how he keeps you. It is a disgrace."

Georgina's brown eyes looked incredulously at the squire. "You are very much mistaken!"

"Don't tell me you are in love with the fellow? God's blood, a woman like you must be more practical. A man like myself would take far better care of you. You're very accomplished, you know. Why, a man would almost mistake you for a lady of quality."

"How dare you say such things to me, you ill-mannered provincial nobody! I was mad to come here."

Georgina turned angrily, but Allenby leapt to his feet and caught her arm. "Provincial nobody, am I? And who is your Mr. Botts? A great gentleman of town, I suppose."

"Were he a . . . a footman, he is a better man than you! Now release me, sir, or you shall regret it."

Allenby tightened his grasp on her arm. "I shall not release you. No, indeed, ma'am, I've never met a wench who amused me so."

"I warn you I shall scream."

"Scream if you wish. There's no one to come to your rescue. I'll only be forced to bruise that pretty face of yours."

"You wouldn't dare touch me."

Allenby laughed. "By God, I would. Try my patience any further, and you shall find that out. Now, you sit down. Over at that table." He shoved her roughly toward an oaken table cluttered with dirty glasses and strewn with playing cards.

Georgina rubbed her arm and obediently sat down. Squire Allenby was possibly mad, and obviously dangerous. What folly it had been for her to come here! If only Sam would come.

"I've not much company here," continued Allenby. "And I could use a woman like you. I've never had a proper mistress, you see. Father was so very straitlaced. I've had to make do with the ladies of the town, but now that I'm master here, I should have a woman—a pretty one like you—to take care of me. I can be a generous man if treated right, and I'll see you have gowns, and jewels for that pretty neck of yours."

The squire was looking at her with a wild expression that made Georgina suddenly terrified. "You mistake me, sir. I am a lady of consequence with important connections at court."

"Are you? Is that why you ride about the countryside on a half-dead nag, dressed like a baker's wife?" He leaned toward her and grasped her hand. "You're a good-looking woman, you are. How about showing a gentleman a bit of fun?"

It took Georgina all her strength to remain calm, and she looked quickly from Allenby to the door and then down at the table. Spying the playing cards, she desperately snatched one up in her free hand. "You play cards, sir?"

"Cards?" He released her hand. "I hardly had cards in mind."

"But I should enjoy a game," she said, with a remarkable coolness bred of desperation. "You are a sporting man, I trust."

"I am, indeed, if the stakes are high enough to be interesting."

Allenby started to collect all the cards. "Wouldn't mind a game or two. There's plenty of time for other pleasures. I warn you, though, Mrs. Botts, there's not a man this side of London can best Robert Allenby at cards, or at much else."

Georgina managed a faint smile. "If I win, sir, I expect you to allow me to leave. And . . ." She paused. "You will allow the Parkers to stay on their land for five years rent free."

A loud guffaw escaped Allenby's lips. "You're a strange one, Mrs. Botts. Very well, but since it is more likely that I will win, I should like to know what I shall have of you if I am the victor."

Georgina frowned. "My horse."

"Your horse? You make me laugh. Let us say, my dear, that if you win it is as you say, and if I win . . . you will stay here with me."

Georgina looked into Allenby's face and wondered how long it would be before Sam came in search of her. "As you wish, squire," she said, finally.

He nodded happily and began to shuffle the cards.

Lord Renwick, under his noble father's watchful eye, had directed into an interest in agriculture the youthful energies most gentlemen of his rank devoted to sport, fashion, and vice. His knowledge of livestock, gained by working with his father's herds of sheep and cattle, was extensive, and he soon impressed Mr. Parker and Will Martin with his sharp eye and practical advice.

Will Martin, who was not one to blithely accept suggestions from strangers, was nevertheless persuaded that the young man from the north knew a great deal about sheep. He listened intently as Renwick examined some of the animals and barraged him with questions. It was, therefore, nearly two hours later when Renwick returned to the Parker house, and he suspected that Lady Georgina would be more than a little perturbed by his tardiness.

When he arrived and found her gone, he was quite astonished; when told that she had gone off shortly after he had left, he was puzzled.

"She said she'd take a little ride, Mr. Botts, but I thought she would have come back long before this."

"Which way did she go, Mrs. Parker?"

"Down the road, toward the squire's house."

"The squire's house?"

"Aye, but she knows where it is and won't go near it. She asked me in particular where the house was so she could avoid it."

"She did, did she?" Renwick frowned. No, he told himself, she would not have gone to see Allenby by herself. Or would she? Renwick's frown grew deeper.

"Well, I shall take my leave of both of you and find her," said Renwick, quickly saying his good-byes and then fetching his horse. As he started off down the road, he was filled with foreboding. The little fool, he thought. I'll wager she has gone off to see that villain Allenby. Probably thought she could charm him into submission. The meddling little idiot. Renwick urged his horse into a canter. "By God, if he's done anything to offend her, I'll kill him."

It was easy to find the squire's house, and Renwick jumped off his horse as the footman came forward to take his reins. He pushed aside the butler at the door, demanding forcefully where to find Squire Allenby. The surprised servant gestured toward the drawing room, and Renwick hurried toward it and thrust open the door.

"Sam!" Georgina was standing over the squire, who was writing something on a paper. Allenby looked up.

"You! Thank God. Come to take back this wench of yours. Good riddance, I say."

"Georgina! What has possessed you to come here?"

Lady Georgina's relief at seeing him was so great that she hardly noticed his familiar use of her name. "Sam, how glad I am to see you!"

Renwick frowned ominously. "What did you think to accomplish by this foolhardiness?"

"Foolhardiness, Sam?" Georgina smiled and took the paper that Allenby had been writing. "You will see I have been most successful." She handed the paper to Renwick, who read it and then looked at Georgina.

"By heaven, the Parkers have five years more rent free!"

"Damn them," muttered Allenby, "and this conniving wench who bested me in every game of cards we played. She had the devil's own luck, and a steadier hand than any I've seen. By the gods, she's an unnatural female, and you're welcome to her. Now get out, the both of you."

Renwick did not much like Allenby's manner, but Georgina took his arm and propelled him quickly out the door and thence out of the house. The marquis was ready to admonish Georgina, but she silenced him with the admission, "Oh, Sam, I was so stupid to come here. That man is horrible."

Renwick stopped and looked down at her. "Did he say or do anything improper? I'll break his neck if he did."

Georgina looked up into Renwick's face and was surprised at the deadly seriousness reflected in his blue eyes. She smiled. "No, my gallant Sam, but let us hurry away from this place and that odious man. And I pray you, do not chide me for coming. I know now that it was ridiculous to do so."

Renwick shook his head, realizing that he had no more wish to rebuke her, but, instead, an urge to pull her close and bury his face in her luxuriant dark hair. This rather startling realization caused the marquis to stare awkwardly at her ladyship, who was puzzled by his discomfiture.

"There are the horses, Sam. I thank providence that my father taught me so many card games. I know Rumbridge thinks it terribly unladylike of me to be proficient at games of chance, but it has stood me in good stead today."

Renwick made no reply, but helped Georgina onto her horse and then mounted his own. He was in an oddly reflective mood, and Georgina made no further attempt at conversation.

They rode back to the Parkers' house, and Georgina presented the astounded couple with Allenby's paper and then wrote down Victor Ballanville's London address, telling the Parkers to contact her through that gentleman if any problems occurred. After being thanked profusely by Mr. and Mrs. Parker, finally Georgina and Renwick were able to break away and resume their journey.

As they rode on, it was Georgina's turn to grow thoughtful.

"What are you thinking about, Lady Georgina? Squire Allenby?"

"Certainly not. I was thinking of America."

"America?"

"Mrs. Parker told me about it. A man's rank is not so important there, you see."

"I think it odd that a lady in your position would find America so appealing."

"And I find it odd that a man in your position would find it unappealing. Have you no wish to better yourself, Sam?"

Renwick could not keep from bursting into laughter, and Georgina frowned at him. "What is so funny?"

"Nothing, my lady."

"So you are, after all, very content at being a servant, Sam. I had thought you ambitious, but it seems I was wrong."

A mischievous look came to Renwick's face. "Ambition is a dangerous trait, my lady. I am merely content to follow in the footsteps of my father."

"And was your father in service?"

"Well, let us say he is associated with many who are in

service on a very large estate in the north." Renwick grinned, and Georgina shook her head.

"Is he a gamekeeper, then?"

"No, although he does have some interest in game."

"I feel as though you are talking in riddles, Sam Botts. And it seems you have become decidedly jovial."

Renwick laughed. "I must admit I am beginning to enjoy myself, Lady Georgina."

"And I must admit, Sam Botts, that I do not understand you at all."

Sam Botts only grinned again.

15

THE CALLS OF SEA BIRDS AND THE SCENTS OF the sea were very welcome to Lady Georgina, who dearly loved the coast but spent little time there. She was also glad to see their journey ending and was eager to see her beloved Miss Liddcott again.

Huntley-on-Sea was a delightful little coastal village, yet undiscovered by the fashionable set. It was inhabited mainly by fishermen, who through hard work coaxed a living from the unwilling sea. It was here that Sophronia Liddcott was born, and here that she returned after spending forty years teaching the children of the well-to-do. She was well known and well regarded in the village, and the first person that Georgina and Renwick met was happy to point out the way to Miss Liddcott's cottage.

The cottage was about a mile distant from town and a pleasant ride along the cliffs that bordered the sea. As they came upon the tiny house, Georgina smiled. "It's Liddy! There, you see her?"

There, working in a garden, was a tall woman wearing a broad sunbonnet. She stopped and watched them as they approached. Georgina pulled up her horse and leapt down with an agility that amazed the marquis.

"Liddy!" she cried. "It is I, Georgina!"

The tall woman looked puzzled for a moment. "Not Lady Georgie!" she cried, with a look of astonishment; and Georgina laughed and, throwing her arms about her, hugged her tightly.

"Oh, Liddy, I have missed you so!"

"I cannot believe it!" said Miss Liddcott as she extricated herself from Georgina's embrace. "It *is* my lady Georgie. Oh, how well you look!"

The marquis got down from his horse and, while he stood by, studied Miss Liddcott. She was very tall, several inches taller than Georgina; and the broad brim of the sunbonnet shaded a thin face with grey eyes that peered over a pair of spectacles. The spectacles rested on what was Miss Liddcott's most noticeable feature, a very long and prominent nose, which, combined with her slightly protruding front teeth and slightly receding chin, made a rather disharmonious picture. However, Miss Liddcott's countenance, although lacking in beauty, was most intelligent and good natured, and the marquis was inclined to like her from the first.

"Oh, Liddy, I must introduce Mr. Botts to you."

Miss Liddcott smiled graciously at Renwick. "Very good to meet you, sir. Oh, I cannot believe this. Lady Georgie and a gentleman come here to see me." She looked again at Renwick and then at Georgina. "You haven't come to say you've been married? Oh, how wonderful!"

"Dear Liddy, I am no such thing!" cried Georgina.

"You are not?" Miss Liddcott looked disappointed. "Oh, I had thought Mr. Botts was the lucky man."

"Oh, Liddy, Mr. Botts would not think himself very lucky at all." She directed a wry smile at him. "No, indeed. Mr. Botts had kindly consented to escort me here. You see, Liddy, I have flown off."

"Flown off!"

"Run away from Rumbridge. I pray you, do not be shocked. My brother is insufferable, as you know."

"But what will you do?"

"I have no idea whatsoever. But let us talk of other things. You are looking so very well, Liddy. I knew from your letter that you were very happy."

"Oh, I am well enough, but it is you I must hear about. Do come in, and I shall fix some tea. You must be exhausted."

Miss Liddcott ushered them into her cottage. It was small, but cozy, and filled with unusual furnishings and works of art that reflected Miss Liddcott's eclectic and rather eccentric tastes. Most prominent among her possessions was an enormous wooden chair carved elaborately with interwining vines and sinuous dog-headed serpents. This, Miss Liddcott hastily pointed out, was the work of a most talented sixteenth century artisan.

She was easily sidetracked into discussing the chair and another prized possession, a bronze disc marked with curious symbols, which she informed them was an ancient navigational device called an astrolabe. Since both Georgina and Renwick seemed quite interested, Miss Liddcott elaborated on the history of the ancient instrument; and then, satisfied that her listeners were suitably impressed, she led them to a small alcove where she triumphantly revealed her pride and joy.

"It is a telescope," said Georgina, eyeing it with surprise.

"Yes," said Miss Liddcott. "And I constructed it myself, with the aid of Mr. Courtenay. And I have seen Uranus!"

Since Renwick had never heard of Uranus, this pronouncement did not impress him overmuch, but Georgina seemed delighted, and the marquis tried to manage an appropriate amount of enthusiasm. Miss Liddcott continued to discuss her telescope, and it did not take long for the marquis to conclude that she was a most unusual lady. Renwick also reflected that Lady Georgina's strong and independent character had doubtless been influenced by Miss Liddcott—and concluded that one would do well to look carefully into the matter of suitable governesses for one's children.

The discussion did not return to Georgina until some time later, when they sat down to tea. After offering them some sugar biscuits, Miss Liddcott abruptly turned the conversation to the "current plight" and asked, "And so, Lady Georgie, what are we to do?"

"I am not sure, Liddy."

"What do you think, Mr. Botts?"

The marquis was rather surprised that Miss Liddcott wanted his opinion. "I believe, ma'am, that Lady Georgina must return to London. What else is there to do?"

"I cannot go back," replied Georgina firmly.

Miss Liddcott looked thoughtful. "It is very difficult. Lord Rumbridge will be very upset, and I expect he shall come after you. Rumbridge may not be the most personable of gentlemen, but he is not a fool, by any means. He shall soon realize where you have gone."

"Oh, it may be some time before he thinks of you, Liddy. And by that time I shall have gone."

"Gone where?" said Miss Liddcott.

"Perhaps to France. My cousin Richard is in Paris, and I could cross from Dover. We are so close here."

"Oh, I have never approved of the French," said Miss Liddcott dubiously.

"Or perhaps I could sail for America. I learned all about it today from a man we met on the road."

"One must be skeptical about things one hears on public roads, Lady Georgie," admonished Miss Liddcott. "And America is a very long way away."

"America," muttered Renwick. "That is the most bird-witted idea!"

"Bird-witted! I have had enough of your impudence, Sam Botts. You have no right to speak to me so."

"Perhaps I don't, my fine lady Georgina. Perhaps I'd best tend to the horses." Renwick got up, murmured "Excuse me" to Miss Liddcott, and left them.

"Oh, dear."

"Don't worry, Liddy. Sam has these bouts of temper. He is a difficult man."

"But you are rather fond of him, are you not?"

Georgina regarded Miss Liddcott with a bewildered expression. "Why would you say that?"

"Oh, I just thought it when I first saw you two. I like that man; I don't quite know why. He seems a nice gentleman."

"But he is not precisely a gentleman, Liddy."

"I don't know of his birth," said Miss Liddcott, "but he has the air of a gentleman, and the look."

"Oh, Liddy, I pray you, stop saying such silly things. And even if Sam Botts were at all suitable, he dislikes me heartily. Oh, perhaps I have given him reason, but I assure you he has an antipathy toward me that I have rarely engendered in anyone. Indeed, we quarrel most of the time."

"A pity," said Miss Liddcott, who was trying to remember the name of a gentleman of high rank she once met who resembled Sam Botts. It was some thirty years past in London, and she only met him briefly. He had later shocked society in that city by running off with one of its most fashionable ladies. However, the name of this gentleman escaped Miss Liddcott, and she soon gave up trying to think of it.

They spent the evening surveying the stars with Miss Liddcott's telescope, and then they retired early. The marquis found accommodations in a tiny room that would have housed a maid had Miss Liddcott been able to afford a full-time servant. The room featured a cot too small for his lordship's large frame, but Renwick was so exhausted that he slept soundly.

Georgina, despite having a quite acceptable bed, had difficulty falling asleep. The cause of this troublesome failure was Sam Botts. She could not keep from thinking about him, and she could not force the image of his handsome face from her mind. It especially infuriated her that what she kept recalling was the memory of his arms around her when he had rescued her at The Fighting Bear. Idiot, she thought to herself. He is only a footman, after all; and yet, footman or no, he troubled her thoughts as no man had done ever before.

She finally fell into a restless sleep, and awakened early. Despite a tendency toward impulsiveness, Georgina was not one to disregard the consequences of her actions. She lay awake in her bed and thought over her options, concluding that she had very few choices. America was not a reasonable solution. She had no money, nor had she friends or relations there. France was possible, but she had no wish to join her cousin's family. No matter how much she would have liked to do so, she could not stay at Huntley-on-Sea. Her brother would find her soon; and even if he didn't, she could not expect to stay long with her former governess, a lady having barely enough to support herself.

"It seems I must return and face Rumbridge," sighed Georgina, "and I shall be married as soon as possible." She smiled as she thought of Milford and decided that he would not want her after hearing of her running off. Indeed, all society had probably heard of it by now, for these things could never be kept quiet. Sir Swithin Baxter would still have her. She was certain of that, and resolved that if she could come up with no better prospect—and she doubted that she could—she would marry Baxter.

Although this was hardly a decision that could bring her joy, Georgina resigned herself to it and felt relieved that she had come up with the answer. She dressed herself in a faded cotton dress that Miss Liddcott had found for her. It was scarcely better than the poor garment borrowed from Sally, but it was clean and fitted her well. She looked into the small mirror on Miss Liddcott's dressing table. Frowning at the state of her hair, she began to brush her dark tresses. When she decided that she had done her best, she came out to greet Miss Liddcott.

That redoubtable lady was busy preparing breakfast. She was proud of her skill in the kitchen despite the fact that cooking skill was not an enviable achievement for ladies on the fringes of upper-class society.

"Good morning, dear Liddy."

"Oh, Lady Georgina, you have risen early."

"You were the one who said one must rise early, for there were too many things to learn to stay abed."

"Oh, I did say that," said Miss Liddcott, patting the dough for scones with floured hands. "I was a terror as a governess."

"You were a wonderful governess."

Miss Liddcott beamed at the praise. "You were the best of my charges, Georgina. But we shall have breakfast very soon. Do sit down, or if you like, take a walk along the sea."

"Oh, I shall stay here and chat with you. We have so much to talk about." Georgina sat down in a chair. "Where is Sam?"

"Oh, he's gone already."

"Gone?" Georgina was dumbfounded. Had he left without a word of good-bye?

"Oh, he's not gone far. He took that horse of yours to the village. One of her shoes was loose. And he was going to see the barber. I must say he was in some need of his services. I do like that young man. He's very kind and considerate."

"Is he? I am amazed to hear it. But Liddy, I have made a decision. I am returning to London."

Miss Liddcott nodded. "I imagined you would do so.

You were always reasonable, after you had calmed down a bit."

"And I will get married. Really, Liddy, it is tedious to have to get married. You are fortunate."

"Oh, I am happy enough, I suppose, but you are a lady of high rank, Georgina, and must think of your duty. And marriage to a kind man of sensitivity and common sense is a very good thing."

"I'm sure it is, but although Swithin Baxter is kind in his silly way, he is neither sensitive nor sensible."

"Not Sir Swithin Baxter, the friend of your late father? Lady Georgie, he is scarcely the man for you!"

"Don't be shocked, Liddy. I assure you it will not be so bad."

"I do not like this," said Miss Liddcott sternly. "I do not like your agreeing to marry such a man. It is outrageous. But I do not doubt his lordship your brother approves of the match."

"Oh, do give him some credit, Liddy. He opposes it, but I'm sure he can be persuaded to agree. When I return I will have achieved a scandalous reputation, and Rumbridge would not care who I married."

Miss Liddcott shook her head and put her scones over the fire. "I don't like it at all. Not at all."

Georgina turned the discussion away from her return to London; and they discussed instead the weather, which had grown threatening, and the village of Huntley-on-Sea, which had grown not at all. Miss Liddcott was very glad that her beloved village had not gone the way of Brighton, the seaside town that the Prince of Wales had transformed from fishing village into fashionable resort filled with hotels, shops, and social climbers.

Just as Miss Liddcott was decrying the sad state of affairs in Brighton, Renwick returned. He knocked at the door and then entered, and Georgina noted a bit resentfully that he looked extremely handsome and in very good spirits.

"Is Matilda all right, Sam?"

"She's a wonder, she is. She needed a new shoe, was all."

"Thank you, Sam, for seeing to it."

"Always eager to help your ladyship," said Renwick, adding the sardonic grin that always irritated her. He then turned to Miss Liddcott. "It's a fine village, and everyone was most helpful—that is, when I told them I was Miss Liddcott's distant relation. I hope you don't mind."

"Indeed not, young man. I shouldn't mind a relation such as you. We were just about to have some scones. They're ready, I think."

Renwick, hungry as usual, was happy to find Miss Liddcott's scones waiting for him and ate with relish, although Georgina was eyeing him disapprovingly.

"Lady Georgina's going back to London."

Miss Liddcott's abrupt comment surprised Renwick, who looked over at Georgina. "You're going back?" Georgina nodded.

"And she's going to be married."

"Liddy! This is no concern of Sam's."

"Married? Not to Milford!"

Georgina was puzzled at his belligerent tone. "No, I don't think he'd have me. I'm going to marry Swithin Baxter."

"Baxter?" Renwick was unsure who Baxter was, and then a flash of recognition hit him. "Good God! Not the doddering old fool who wagered against me?"

"I should not call him doddering."

Renwick looked incredulously at her. "The man's an idiot, and old enough to be your father."

"And he is also very rich and will allow me to do as I please."

Renwick was suddenly angry. "I might have known you would decide something like this. Of course, marry an old fool and continue your gay life as one of the prince's paramours."

"How dare you!" Georgina was furious. "You don't know anything about the prince, and you don't know anything about me. It appears, Liddy, it is my turn to depart." Georgina stormed out of the cottage, leaving Renwick to shake his head.

"How could she marry Baxter?"

"I think, sir, that you are hard on her. Of course she does not want to marry Baxter; but does she have a choice?"

"The little fool has the choice of any man in England. I believe she cares only for her position as 'friend' of His Royal Highness."

Miss Liddcott raised her eyebrows. "My dear sir, I have never heard anything so utterly ridiculous in my life. Georgina has known the prince from childhood and has always been fond of him, but you must be very green indeed if you do not realize that His Royal Highness's taste runs to more mature women. And if you believe *my* Lady Georgina would become one of the prince's mistresses, I fear you do not know her very well."

The marquis had not expected this spirited defense and was quite chagrined. "I am a fool," he murmured awkwardly.

"You are jealous. That is all. You love her yourself."

"Miss Liddcott!"

She smiled and pushed her spectacles up on her nose. "Do you deny it?" He paused in confusion. "No, of course not. I may be seem an addled old maid, but I have a quick eye and I know what I'm about. You'd do well to go after her and apologize. She's very fond of you."

"That's nonsense. She could never think of me except as a meddlesome servant."

"Indeed? I know this lady, sir, and I tell you that you are very wrong."

This comment startled Renwick. He got up and, without another word, rushed out to find Georgina. He looked toward the beach and saw her vanish down the path that led to the sea. The wind was up and the sky was growing black, and as he climbed down the path from the cliff, he heard the roar of the sea as great waves battered the shore.

It had grown suddenly cold, and Renwick looked warily at the sky. There was one lone boat out upon the water, and it bobbed up and down upon the choppy waters as it struggled to return to land before the storm broke in fury.

"Georgina!" he shouted, but the rush of the waves drowned out his voice. He increased his speed, breaking into a run as he got to the beach, at the bottom of the cliff. "Georgina!"

She heard him this time and turned her head, but continued walking. He caught up with her a few moments later.

"Come back. It's going to rain and it's cold. I'm sorry."

Georgina continued walking.

"It's cold. You'll freeze to death."

She kept walking, and he followed after her. "Don't be a fool!"

"More insults, then?" she shouted, and increased her pace.

"Damn," muttered Renwick. "Stop and listen to me!"

The rain began to fall, and they were soaked immediately. "Dammit, Georgina!" shouted Renwick in frustration. He grabbed her arm and pulled her to him. "Stop this nonsense!"

She tried to pull her arm away, but he held it fast; and she looked defiantly up at him. "What now, Sam? Are you going to beat me?"

"Dammit, woman! Can't you be reasonable? Good God, we're getting soaked. You shall catch your death of cold in that dress."

"And why should you care!" shouted Georgina, suddenly bursting into tears and trying to jerk her arm away from his grasp.

"Goddammit!" he shouted. "I *do* care. I'm in love with you!" He was nearly as surprised as she was at the words. "It's true," he shouted again. "If I've acted like an ass, it's because I love you. By God, Georgina, I love you desperately."

Her dark eyes expressed disbelief, and then wonder. "Oh, Sam."

Two strong arms enveloped her, and Georgina found herself crushed in his embrace, his lips pressing against hers with a passion that overwhelmed them both.

"Sam, darling Sam," she murmured as their lips parted. "I love you, too." He replied by kissing her again, with renewed fervor, and Georgina found her body stirring with strange and yet delightful sensations. The marquis somehow came to his senses and, pulling off his coat, drew it about her shoulders.

"This is no place for us," he said, as the rain pounded against their faces. "Come." Taking her by the hand, he led her to the base of the cliff, which offered some protection from the rain that was now coming down in torrents.

"Let's go back to the house. You must dry off."

Georgina nodded, but threw her arms around him again. "Oh, Sam, I couldn't admit to myself how I felt. I do love you—but what are we to do?"

"Get married, of course," he said, embracing her tightly.

"Then I should really become Mrs. Botts, after all."

Renwick looked startled. "Good God, I had forgotten. You would marry Sam Botts, a footman?"

"Yes, I would. Perhaps I am mad, but I don't think so. We could go to America, Sam, where titles count for nothing."

"Unfortunately, my sweet, I doubt that there is a place, even America, where titles count for nothing."

She looked up at him in surprise.

"Georgina, I love you very much, and I want you to marry me. But I have a confession to make to you."

"A confession?"

"Yes. You see, I am not what you think I am. I am not who you think I am."

"What do you mean?"

"I mean—" His words were stopped by another sound. Above the tumultuous noise of the sea, there was a faint cry.

Georgina heard it too. "Look, Sam, a boat!"

The small fishing vessel Renwick had seen before had foundered upon the shore, and they could hear the snapping of wood as the boat was tossed upon the rocks. The rain made it difficult to see, and Renwick strained his eyes to find two crew members struggling against the waves.

"Georgina, wait here and watch the boat. I'll run for help." Renwick rushed up to Miss Liddcott's cottage and found that lady nearly sick with worry.

"There's a boat wrecked on the shore," shouted Renwick. "I'll need a strong rope. Would you have one?" Miss Liddcott nodded, and they hurried to the small shed outside, where they found a sturdy line. "Any help nearby?"

"Not until the village."

"Don't worry. Just stay here!"

Renwick ran out, the line slung over his shoulder, and hurried off to the beach. Miss Liddcott wrung her hands fearfully, and then trained her faithful telescope upon the sea.

"There, Sam, it's breaking up," cried Georgina. "They'll be washed away!"

Renwick surveyed the beach and found a rocky promontory extending from the cliff bottom. He tied one end around the rocky projection and the other around his waist, and then proceeded to wade into the sea.

"Oh, Sam! Be careful."

The waves rose above his head, and he struggled to maintain his footing, but was many times knocked over by the force of the waves. He kept on and, after what seemed an eternity, reached the wreckage, where two men clung tenaciously to what was left of the boat. Renwick's great strength was fortified by the emergency, and he helped the two from the boat.

One of them was hurt, but the other was able to grasp the line and began to pull himself toward the shore. Grasping the other man firmly around the waist, Renwick started back. Buffeted by the waves and hampered by the man's deadweight, Renwick struggled fiercely toward shore. A great wave knocked him off his feet, and he choked on a mouthful of briny water and lost hold of the man he was trying to rescue. He reached out wildly, grabbed him again, and continued on.

The few more yards to safety seemed like miles, but finally Renwick, with his inert burden, collapsed on the shore. Georgina and the other man from the boat hurried to help them.

"Sam! Sam!"

"I'm all right," Renwick assured Georgina, and turned to the man he had been carrying.

"Billy!" called the other man, slapping the inert form of his companion. "Billy, come on, then." Renwick was not at all optimistic, for Billy showed no sign of life.

"Please, Billy," called the other man, bursting into tears of helplessness. Renwick pushed him aside and turned Billy onto his stomach. He pushed tentatively on the man's back. Suddenly there was a sign of life, and the man coughed and then coughed again, expelling a great quantity of water.

"Praise God," cried the other man.

Renwick unfastened the line from around his waist. Then, hoisting the recovering Billy onto his shoulders, he carried him up the path to Miss Liddcott's cottage.

Miss Liddcott expressed great joy at their return and hurried to add fuel to the fire and wrap them all in blankets. Georgina was hastily commanded to change her clothes, which she did quite willingly. The others huddled around the fire. "Lord, Miss Liddcott," said the now revived Billy. "We'd o' been gone for certain had this gentleman not pulled us out."

"Aye," nodded the other.

"Mr. Botts," said Miss Liddcott, "it appears you've saved Billy Weekes and his brother Daniel."

The Weekes brothers thanked Renwick profusely, vowing that Sam Botts, as he introduced himself, was the greatest man alive and they'd have no way of repaying him, but if they could do anything at all, they would do it gladly.

Renwick, embarrassed by all this gratitude, muttered that he was only glad he could help. Georgina had changed and returned to the room, where she sat beside Renwick and looked fondly at him. "I was so worried," she whispered.

"No need to worry, my love," he whispered back. "I was not about to depart this world now that we have discovered each other."

It was not at all easy to keep from kissing him, but Georgina restrained herself, since she had no wish to shock Miss Liddcott or the two brothers.

The rain ended as suddenly as it had begun, and Daniel Weekes said they must return before everyone would think them dead. They were not yet fully recovered from their ordeal, and Renwick offered to take them back to the village in Miss Liddcott's pony cart.

After hitching Miss Liddcott's horse to the cart, the marquis helped the two brothers into the cart and was off to the village. Renwick said good-bye and pressed Georgina's hand, saying he had to finish his "confession."

Georgina had forgotten all about this in the confusion, but she nodded at Sam as he took his leave, and returned to the house with Miss Liddcott. Confession, she thought uneasily. Could he have been in prison? She smiled, reflecting that even if he had, it would be scarcely more shocking than the fact that he was a servant and she, the daughter of an earl, had agreed to marry him.

"What is it, Lady Georgie? You are so pensive."

"Oh, Liddy, I believe I have exchanged one set of troubles for another. And yet I am so very happy. I don't even know if I can tell you. You will be very shocked."

Miss Liddcott seemed willing to risk being shocked, and Georgina continued. "I am going to marry Sam Botts. I believe it will be the most scandalous event of the year."

"Oh, Georgie, you shall be happy. I do like this Sam."

"But you don't understand, Liddy. Sam may act like a gentleman, and he is as noble a man as has ever lived, but he is not a gentleman. He is a servant in the employ of Victor Ballanville."

"Ballanville!" Miss Liddcott looked as though she remembered something. "That's it. Ballanville!"

"You see, there was a wager to try to make Sam into a gentleman. It was a joke of sorts, and a bad one."

"Are you sure he is not a gentleman? He appears—"

"Oh, I know how he appears. But the fact remains he is Sam Botts—and I don't care at all."

A knock at the door startled them both. "Is Sam back already?" cried Georgina, hurrying to the door. She flung it open, and a look of astonishment came to her face. There stood her brother, the Earl of Rumbridge, with a most inhospitable expression on his face.

16

THE MARQUIS OF RENWICK SOON DISCOVERED that tearing oneself away from the family of two men whose lives have just been saved is no easy task. Billy Weekes's wife wept for joy, and his mother lifted her hands toward the heavens and prayed that blessings might be heaped upon Renwick's head.

The Weekes brothers lived in a crowded little house with their parents, Billy's wife and infant daughter, and three other brothers and sisters. They insisted that Renwick relate the adventure and then have a drink of the good rum they had been saving for a celebration.

One of the younger Weekes brothers rushed out to tell the neighbors, and soon the house was crowded with villagers who wanted to see the stranger who had saved two of their own. Renwick received many slaps on the back and hearty good wishes, and he desperately wished he could get back to Georgina. Finally, he was able to break away, saying he must get back to Miss Liddcott's house, and the well-wishers reluctantly allowed him to leave only after he swore he would return again before he returned north. Thus, finally escaping from the flood of gratitude, Renwick hurried back to the cottage.

He was rather uneasy about telling Georgina the truth. Why had he not done so earlier? Yet, he reasoned, if she was willing to marry lowly Sam Botts, perhaps she would accept him as heir to a dukedom. He smiled at the absurdity of it and then grew wistful as he thought of Georgina soaking wet and, while he held her close, saying she loved him. Renwick whipped the horse impatiently. When he arrived at the cottage, he hurried to unharness the cart horse.

He entered the cottage and looked expectantly around the now empty room. "Georgina?"

Miss Liddcott appeared, a worried expression on her face. "She's gone."

"Gone? What do you mean?"

"Just after you left, the Earl of Rumbridge arrived."

"The devil!"

"Indeed, he seemed very like the devil himself. He was outraged and would not listen to Georgina at all. He had two of his men with him, and he threatened to toss her forcibly into his carriage."

"By my honor, I will break his neck."

"Calm yourself, sir. You will return to London and make matters right. And quickly, too! She is very much in love with you. So much so that she would abandon her station and marry a mere footman."

Renwick looked rather uncomfortable.

"Out with it, sir," said Miss Liddcott sternly. "You are no footman! I knew it from the first. It is a cruel game you are playing, sir. And if it is your wish to hurt my lady, you shall regret it."

Renwick frowned. "I love her with all my heart, and I would never hurt her, but it is a very long story."

"You are a Ballanville, are you not? You bear a most uncanny resemblance to a young marquis I met in London thirty years ago. He was heir to a dukedom, as I recall."

Renwick smiled ruefully. "As I am. I am Hugh Ballanville, Marquis of Renwick, and you must have met my father, the Duke of Welham."

"Good heavens! And Georgina thinks you are a footman. I daresay, sir, you must explain how this came about."

Renwick nodded and began his explanation.

The ride back to London in her brother's carriage was one of the most unpleasant experiences of Georgina's life. Rumbridge was so furious with her that he would not even speak to her, and she responded by adopting a detached sullen look and made no attempt to talk to him. They arrived at the London townhouse just as it was growing dark, and Rumbridge led her inside. Her sister-in-law was there to greet them. "Oh, Georgina," Amelia cried. "How could you have done this to us?" Receiving no response from Georgina, Amelia turned to her husband.

"Where did you find her, Rumbridge? At the home of this Miss Liddcott?"

"Yes, and I had to nearly drag her to the carriage."

"Oh, Georgina, what will we do now? Oh, and you look so dreadful, too."

"May I go now?" Georgina looked resentfully at her brother and his wife.

"No, I don't think so. Sit down in the drawing room. We must settle some things. By my honor, Amelia, I could not trust myself to speak before."

Georgina shrugged and sat down on the drawing room sofa, and readied herself for Rumbridge's tirade.

"Never," he began, folding his arms across his chest and looking sternly at her, "has such a scandal blighted our family name. I knew our father's indulgence with you would have serious consequences. You became spoiled and willful and lost all sense of propriety and duty.

"You have been a source of pain to me since our father's death. You have consistently flaunted my authority and consorted with immoral persons, from fashionable debauchees to actors.

"But now, dear sister, you have caused a scandal of enormous proportions by stealing from this house in disguise and running off. You have been gone for two nights, my girl, and try as we did, we could not keep such things secret. There is not a person in society who does not know of this by now, and you are ruined. Completely ruined. No gentleman would ever marry you now."

"I care nothing for gentlemen if they are all as smug and sanctimonious as you, Rumbridge."

He grew red with rage at this, and she feared for a moment that he would strike her. But he turned abruptly and walked out.

The Countess of Rumbridge frowned. "You would do well to beg my husband's forgiveness. It is not every brother who would take you back."

"Is that what he is doing, Amelia? Taking me back?

Indeed, he dragged me back by brute force. I should have been happy never to see either of you again."

"And do you think I am overjoyed at this reunion? Indeed not, miss, but we must all do our duty, and mine is to help my husband preserve the family name. I have my sons to think of! And like it or not, Georgina, you will try to lend some respectability to your behavior."

"I, respectable? Surely not, Amelia. But how shall I become respectable after my shocking behavior?"

"That is a problem. But we will start by having you attend Lady Carrington's ball tomorrow as if nothing ever happened."

"Lady Carrington's ball?" Georgina had forgotten all about it. "You are not serious!"

"I am, indeed. Rumbridge and I thought that you must appear to put a stop to the rumors going about town."

"I will not go," said Georgina stubbornly.

"I think you will," said Amelia. "You will go if my husband's men have to drag you. And now I suggest you go to your room. And don't expect to find your Sally. We know her part in this affair, and she has been released from her duties."

"Sally! How could you? She has been with me since before papa died!"

"It is not you who pay her wages, Georgina. Now go to bed."

Georgina glared at her sister-in-law, but felt it useless to protest further. Instead, she got up and retreated to her room, where she flung herself upon her bed and burst into tears. "Oh, Sam," she murmured. "Where are you?"

Brushing a tear aside, she sat up on the bed. Sam Botts was a resourceful man, she reasoned. He would come for her. She must only wait. Heartened by this thought, she got up and began to undress.

Since the carriage had at least two hours' head start, Renwick was unable to catch up with it. He later reflected that this was fortunate, since in his present mood he might have had call to regret his actions.

It was dark when he arrived at Victor's house, and his horse was very tired. Renwick, too, was exhausted as he turned his horse over to Victor's groom and wearily made his way to his cousin's door.

He was met there by Smallbone, who expressed great joy at seeing him. "Praise God, my lord, that you are back."

Smallbone was not given to such exclamations, and Renwick frowned. "What is wrong, Smallbone? Is Victor all right?"

"Mr. Ballanville is well—or as well as can be expected, my lord. You see, his Grace of Welham arrived today."

"What? My father? Here?"

"Yes, my lord. Accompanied by a Sam Botts, I might add."

"Oh, no. Where is he?"

"In the drawing room, and Mr. Ballanville will be much relieved to see you, my lord."

Renwick smiled. "Poor Victor. But I must rescue him, I suppose."

He hurried to the drawing room and entered. Never had anyone been so glad to see him as Victor Ballanville was at that moment. "Here he is now, uncle," cried Victor, leaping to his feet. "Cousin Hugh, so you are back from your visit with old Colonel Blandford. How that man can talk!" Victor grasped his cousin's hand and shook it, whispering, "Thank God you're here, I didn't know what I was going to do."

"Renwick." The Duke of Welham rose from his chair. Though dressed plainly in an unfashionable suit of clothes, His Grace of Welham exuded authority. He was a most formidable personage whose stern eye and dour countenance caused a good many people to feel uncomfortable in his presence. Victor watched the duke and thought he could detect a softening in his uncle's visage when he viewed his son. Indeed, his grace loved all his children dearly and was very proud of his only son.

"Father." Renwick smiled, and then warmly shook his father's hand. "I never expected you, sir. How good to see you. Forgive me, I fear I am not presentable, but when I heard you were here I hurried in. How is everyone at Welham?"

"Well enough," said the duke. "Your sisters send their love. Your nephews miss you."

"Do they? I miss them, too, and I also missed you, father."

His Grace of Welham was not one to indulge in sentimentality. Although he was touched at his son's words and demeanor, he muttered, "Oh, balderdash," and Renwick laughed.

"But why have you come, father? You aren't checking up on me?"

"Don't be absurd. I was thinking it was time I come to London. I thought I might come to young Victor's wedding."

"And I am very glad of that," interjected Victor, but a stern look from his grace told him that no comment was necessary.

"So do you like London?" asked the duke.

"Very much." Seeing his father's look of disappointment, Renwick grinned. "It is exciting when one has never before seen it. And after all my effort in begging you to let me come, father, I should hope I would like it."

A slight smile came to the duke's face, and Victor gave a sigh of relief. His uncle had not smiled once since his arrival, and the change in his expression altered his appearance so much that Victor was able for the first time to see the resemblance between the duke and his son.

"I hope you have not been indulging in frivolity here," said the duke, quickly removing his smile.

"Certainly not, sir," said Renwick.

"And have you had any luck with the business we discussed before you came?"

Victor looked curiously at his cousin and then the duke. "Did my cousin have some business to transact, uncle?"

"The business of finding a wife," said the duke. "Well, did you?"

Victor smiled at his cousin and eagerly awaited his reply.

"Yes, I have, father. I have found the perfect wife."

"You have?" Victor looked at him in astonishment.

Renwick nodded. "Her name is Georgina Suttondale, sister to the Earl of Rumbridge."

"Georgina? Good God, Hugh!" Victor Ballanville had never been more surprised.

"Suttondale," said the duke. "Good family, though the fourth earl was a wild one, if I recollect."

"But the present earl is the very picture of sobriety," said Victor. He turned again to Renwick. "Lady Georgina, Hugh?"

"Then you know this girl, Victor?"

"Of course, uncle. She is cousin to Miss Amesbury, my betrothed. And although she will be an excellent wife for Hugh, I am quite surprised, for Hugh did not confide his choice to me."

"No, Victor, I wanted to address the lady first."

"And what did she say?"

"She seemed most agreeable."

"Good," said the duke. "I shall be eager to meet the lady. Suttondale, eh? Seems a good enough choice. But you'll tell me more about her tomorrow. I'm going off to bed. It's getting late."

Victor Ballanville was very relieved to see his uncle retire to bed, for he was eager to question Renwick.

"By God, Hugh, what has happened?" cried Victor as soon as the duke was safely gone. "The entire town is talking about Georgina. Of course, Rumbridge himself is to blame, rushing about town like an idiot searching for her. It seems you have found her—and what is this about marriage? No, wait; I must have my sherry first before you start. Smallbone! Get in here."

After having Smallbone pour their sherry, they both sat down on the sofa, and Victor listened intently to his cousin's tale. Every so often he would interject a "Good God!" or "The devil!" as the marquis related his adventures.

At the conclusion Victor was incredulous. "And she still doesn't know who you are? I cannot believe it! She would marry you even if you were a footman? Good lord!"

"I am more interested in knowing whether she will marry me when she knows who I really am. It's a wretched mess, Vic. But I shall endeavor to see her tomorrow and explain the entire matter."

Victor nodded. "I pray God she forgives us both. It will be a most eventful day tomorrow, my dear Hugh, for in addition to your confession to Georgina, do not forget that it also happens to be Lady Carrington's ball."

"Good God," said Renwick.

17

OF THE MANY EVENTS OF THE LONDON SEAson, Lady Carrington's ball was the affair most eagerly awaited. It was not that Lady Carrington was the most charming of hostesses, for she was heartily disliked in most circles; nor was it the splendor of the Carrington House ballroom, which, although among the finest in London, was not in itself a great attraction. The reason for the ball's popularity was that, after one of them, someone had heard the Prince Regent proclaim that "anyone of any significance in society may be expected to be found there." Thus, persons of significance and those wishing to be persons of significance were most eager to snare invitations. Lady Carrington, well aware of her power, distributed or withheld her invitations with a maddening capriciousness.

Lady Georgina Suttondale was one of the few in London who had no wish to attend the ball. Indeed, she staunchly refused all morning, until it became apparent that her brother could not be swayed from his stand. Then she had surrendered conditionally, saying she would attend only if Sally was restored to her. This being a rather small concession, Rumbridge agreed, and Sally Jenkins was brought back in time to ready her mistress for the ball.

After hours of her maid's careful and painstaking work, Georgina, arrayed in a magnificent gown of ivory satin and her dark hair coiffed and decorated with plumes, was ready to go. Even the Countess of Rumbridge grudgingly admitted to herself that her sister-in-law looked marvelous, and it was with considerable envy that she accompanied her and Rumbridge to their awaiting carriage.

The arrival of the Earl and Countess of Rumbridge and Lady Georgina at Carrington House caused considerable interest. Lady Georgina's arrival always generated much interest, for as she was one of the great beauties of society, everyone was eager to see her gown and how she would wear her hair and which of the gentlemen would act the most foolish in trying to gain her attention. This evening, however, those assembled were especially eager to see Georgina. A rumor had flown about town that she had run off. Some speculated she had eloped with some daring gentleman, but had been forcibly returned to town. Since details of this scandalous event were woefully lacking, most people had to content themselves with inventing their own, and the stories that circulated that evening were most imaginative.

Georgina, although aware of the looks and whispers of the crowd, seemed oblivious to them as she walked into the ballroom with all the grace and dignity of a storybook princess. Lady Carrington afforded the Rumbridge party a most perfunctory greeting, and many others, taking the cue, were standoffish and unwilling to commit themselves to greeting a young woman whose standing in society now seemed rather shaky.

Georgina scanned the ballroom for familiar faces. Has Sam come? was the question foremost in her mind as she looked about, but she was also eager to see Penelope. She spied her cousin and would have hurried to her side, but for Rumbridge's hovering presence. The earl had vowed that he would stay close by her side, and she would have to wait until Penelope came to her.

This Penelope was anxious to do, for she had heard Georgina's arrival announced. However, Miss Amesbury was engaged in conversation with the Dowager Duchess of Winchester, and one did not lightly break off conversation with this redoubtable lady.

"Our reception is rather cold, is it not?" whispered Georgina to her brother.

The earl said sarcastically, "It is to be expected, is it not? Oh, there is Milford."

It was indeed the Viscount Milford, in all his sartorial

elegance, sporting a diamond-encrusted quizzing glass that hung from a velvet ribbon about his neck.

Lord Milford nodded to the countess and then to Rumbridge, and then directed a very cold stare at Georgina. Without so much as a nod, the viscount turned his back and retreated through the crowd. This obvious snub had not gone unnoticed and soon was being widely remarked. That the Lady Georgina was publicly snubbed by the man everyone thought she would marry was a shocking development, and everyone waited eagerly to see what might happen next.

Georgina was furious, and it was with great difficulty that she held her temper and appeared quite unconcerned. Fortunately, a diversion appeared in the form of Richard Averton, accompanied by Swithin Baxter and Mrs. Charles Pendleton. Mrs. Pendleton, a very charming lady, engaged the earl and his countess in conversation. Since Mrs. Pendleton was rumored to be Averton's mistress, she was not the sort of person with whom Rumbridge liked to talk. However, he had little alternative, and since Mrs. Pendleton was a skilled conversationalist, Rumbridge found himself discussing his sons' progress at Eton, where by happy coincidence Mrs. Pendleton's son was also enrolled.

"Bless Edwina," said Averton to Georgina. "She's agreed to help us spirit you away from his lordship. By God, he is grim tonight, and the countess looks as if she is suffering from a toothache."

"Oh, that is how she always looks, Averton," commented Sir Swithin Baxter, taking Georgina's arm. "Let us be off."

"Yes," said Averton with a smile. "We must make our escape while it is still possible." They led a grateful Georgina off to the other end of the ballroom.

"Now you are safe."

"Thank you, Richard, and you, too, Swithin."

Sir Swithin grinned his usual idiotic grin. "'Pon my honor, Georgina, if you ain't the most beautiful girl I've ever seen, I'm a green salamander."

"Why, thank you, Swithin."

"You'll dance with me, won't you, Georgina?"

"Certainly, Swithin. Indeed, I daresay you are the only

man brave enough to dance with me. I fear everyone else thinks me too scandalous."

"Nonsense," said Sir Swithin.

"Indeed," said Averton. "But I am afraid, my dear, that you are the object of much talk this evening. Rumbridge is such a fool that he had not sense enough to keep a discreet silence about the matter." Averton paused. "And I must admit, Georgina, I, too, am wondering about this absence of yours."

"Oh, Richard. Well, I shall tell you all about it, but I must find Sam first. That is, the Marquis of Renwick. Is he here?"

"Renwick? Yes, I did exchange a few words with him."

"He is here?"

"And doing very well, I regret to say," said Swithin Baxter. "Looks as if my three hundred pounds is as good as gone."

"Three hundred pounds?" Richard Averton looked puzzled. He had not heard of the prank and had no idea what Baxter was referring to. "What is this? A wager?"

"Oh, it's a secret for tonight," said Baxter, winking at Georgina.

"Oh, please do not even mention that!"

"Very well, let's talk of something else. Will you marry me, then?"

Averton, although well practiced at not allowing surprise to mar his calm visage, looked astounded. "Good God, Baxter, this is no place to discuss such things!"

However, before Georgina could comment, the arrival of His Royal Highness the Prince Regent was announced. This stopped all conversation and caused everyone present to turn toward the entrance of the ballroom to await the prince's entrance.

The stout form of royal George entered the ballroom, and all of the elegantly dressed ladies and gentlemen made their best bows and curtseys. The prince acknowledged the greeting with a condescending nod, and soon conversation was resumed.

"Prinny's looking well," commented Averton. "I told him that coat looked well. He was a bit skeptical, but fortunately I convinced him. I must say I have never seen him looking better."

Baxter nodded. "Grown stouter though, hasn't he? Pity.

He's in a good mood, though. Who is that he's greeting now? Never seen him before that I remember. Damned shabby appearance he's making."

Georgina watched the prince talking to a grey-haired and very dignified gentleman, who was dressed in an unfashionable evening coat that was years old and contrasted greatly with the exquisitely tailored outfit of the other gentlemen. The elderly man, despite his clothes, had a noble bearing and seemed not at all nervous about conversing with the first gentleman of the land.

"Oh, don't you know?" said Averton, gazing at the man. "That is the Duke of Welham. He's finally come to London after thirty years. The prince appears quite taken with him. I should love to meet him and perhaps could persuade Renwick to introduce me."

"Renwick?" Swithin Baxter looked at Georgina.

"Oh, no," said Georgina weakly.

"Georgina, dearest!" Georgina looked up to see her cousin Penelope, attired in a lovely blue gown. Penelope took her cousin's hands. "Oh, Georgie, I was so worried about you. What has happened to you? Victor and I were so worried."

"Penelope, I can't talk about that now. The Duke of Welham is here. There he is, talking to Prinny. What will we do?"

"What will we do?"

"About Sam, of course!"

"Oh, Georgie. Don't you know? . . ."

"He's in terrible trouble," said Georgina, ignoring her cousin's words. "I must find him. Do excuse me!"

"But wait—" Penelope's words were unheeded as her cousin rushed off.

"What is happening?" said Baxter. "Good Lord, Penelope, this is a devil of a situation. The Duke of Welham here? Good God. This fellow of yours must go."

"What are you talking about?" said Averton impatiently.

"Oh dear," said Penelope. "Poor Richard knows nothing about this. I shall explain, but first, Swithin, there is something I must tell you about Sam Botts."

Georgina hurried across the room, looking everywhere for Renwick. She finally spied him standing by himself, surveying the crowd with a worried look upon his face. They saw each other at the same time. A wide smile came instantly to Renwick's face, and he rushed across the crowded ballroom to her side.

"Georgina," he said, taking both of her hands in his. "My dear Georgina. I have been trying to see you. I came twice to your home today, but your brother's servants refused to admit me!"

"Oh, Sam." Georgina's dark eyes were filled with fear. "You must make haste to leave. I fear there is serious trouble! The Duke of Welham is here. It will be discovered that you are not Renwick and it will be disastrous!"

"Oh, my dear Georgina." It was all Renwick could do to keep from throwing his arms around her and pulling her close, but the presence of all of society made such behavior out of the question. "There is nothing to fear. Oh, Georgina, I tried to tell you about myself the night of the storm. And I would have done so today—"

"What is it, Sam? What do you mean?"

"Georgina, don't hate me. I beg you."

"Don't be absurd, Sam. Hate you? How could I?"

"I pray that is true, my darling, but I have deceived you. I am not Sam Botts. In truth I am—"

The marquis was stopped in midsentence by the appearance of two gentlemen. Georgina looked at them in horror, for they were none other than His Royal Highness the Prince of Wales, and His Grace the Duke of Welham. Georgina felt for a terrible second that she might faint, but she managed to make a presentable curtsey.

"Dear Georgina," said the prince, offering her his hand and helping her to rise. "How beautiful you look! It is not fair that Renwick here should take all of your time."

Georgina tried to smile, but looked fearfully at the duke, waiting for his reaction at hearing this stranger addressed as "Renwick." However, to Georgina's considerable surprise, the duke seemed to find it in no way unusual. "I met your son, Welham," the prince continued, "and was eager to meet you. You have kept young Renwick too long from society."

"Perhaps I have, sir," said the duke. "And I admit I've been wrong."

Had Renwick not been so preoccupied with Georgina, he may have been quite amazed to hear his noble father make this admission, for His Grace of Welham did not make a habit of admitting error.

"And now, Duke, I shall have the pleasure of introducing you to one of society's most charming young ladies, one of the very good reasons that one should not avoid London society. Lady Georgina Suttondale, the Duke of Welham."

Georgina managed another curtsey, and the duke made an old-fashioned bow. "You are the Duke of Welham?"

"Aye," said His Grace. "My son has told me much about you, and I see he shares my good judgment where ladies are concerned."

"Your son? Then this is really Lord Renwick?"

The duke thought this a most peculiar question, and the prince regarded Georgina curiously.

Georgina looked questioningly at Renwick, who nodded. "Yes, I tried to tell you."

The look of astonishment that came to Georgina's face confused the prince. "What is it, Georgina?" he said.

"Oh, forgive me, sir. Oh, please, forgive me. I beg Your Royal Highness to excuse me. Oh, do forgive me, sir." Without waiting for a word from the prince, Georgina raced off, leaving the prince startled and bewildered, and Renwick dismayed.

"Good God," muttered the prince. "What is this about, Renwick? Explain it, sir."

"I beg Your Royal Highness's pardon," said the marquis. "It is my fault. I must go to her. Pray, excuse me, sir." Renwick, too, rushed away, and the prince regarded the duke in alarm.

"By God, Welham, what is going on?"

"I swear to you I do not know, sir," said the duke. "I am so sorry about my son's inexcusable behavior."

"Inexcusable, indeed," said the prince. "There had best be an explanation for this."

"I am certain there is, sir," said the duke, who was appalled at his son. To leave the prince without permission was unheard of and to dash off in such a way was incredible and, in the prince's eyes, akin to treason. Those who had been watching—and there were many who followed the prince's every move—were certain they had never witnessed anything more scandalous. The prince frowned, and everyone watched avidly to see what might happen next.

Only vaguely aware of the furor she had created, Georgina made her way across the ballroom and out into Lady Carrington's garden. The garden was quite deserted, and Georgina collapsed upon a decorative stone bench and covered her face with her hands.

"Georgina!"

"Go away."

"No, I won't go away." Renwick sat down beside her. "I tried to tell you. I did."

"I shall never forgive you. What a fool I have been, and what sport you must have had at my expense! Oh, how you must have laughed when I said I'd marry poor Sam Botts, a footman. Oh, yes, it must have been so very funny."

"Stop this, Georgina. Don't forget you made much sport of me. I regret it now, but I was so angry with you I wanted to teach you a lesson." He grasped her shoulders, and when she tried to pull loose, he grasped her firmly. "Look at me. I say look at me, Georgina." Reluctantly, she lifted her head and met his blue eyes. "I didn't know I was falling in love with you. By heaven, Georgina, I have never been in love before and am so frightfully dim-witted I didn't realize it until that day at Huntley-on-Sea.

"You loved me, too. I know it; and by God if you can love me as Sam Botts I'm damned if I can't see why you can't love me as the Marquis of Renwick!"

She looked at him for a moment, and his expression was so earnest and so angry that she suddenly thought him quite ridiculous.

"And are you truly the Marquis of Renwick?" she said, a trace of a smile betraying her stern tone.

"Of course I am, you vixen," he said, bursting into laughter.

"Oh, Sam." She threw her arms about his neck and kissed him firmly on the lips, an action joyfully reciprocated by the marquis, who crushed her to him and kissed her again and again, and then suddenly pulled back and looked at her quizzically.

"You'll have to call me by my other name. Sam won't really do."

"And what is that name?"

"Hugh. Hugh Charles Glendonwyn St. Ives Ballanville."

"That's a great deal more to remember than Sam Botts, my dearest, but I shall try."

Renwick laughed, and would have kissed Georgina again had not the form of a stout gentleman appeared. Renwick glimpsed this gentleman, and, releasing Georgina, immediately jumped to his feet.

"Your Royal Highness!"

"Your Royal Highness!" repeated Georgina, rising quickly and gazing with alarm at the Prince of Wales, whose face had taken on a dangerously ill-humored expression.

"It's not often that people behave in such a manner in my presence."

"Oh, sir," cried Georgina. "You must forgive us; but no, I am sure our conduct was unforgivable."

A faint smile appeared on the prince's face. "You see, sir, I had been led to believe Lord Renwick was not actually Lord Renwick."

"Indeed?"

"You see, sir, it was all a joke," began Georgina, launching into a lengthy explanation. His Royal Highness was famous for his love of practical jokes and, fortunately, found the story amusing. "And you see, sir," concluded Georgina, "I was so amazed to learn the truth in this way that I lost all reason, even to the point of slighting Your Royal Highness, which, by my faith, I would never have done had I not been so dreadfully muddled."

"Muddled, Georgina?" She nodded up at him, and he could not resist her earnest expression. "Oh, very well, I forgive you." He paused and looked from Georgina to Renwick. "And so it seems by this newfound familiarity that you two will be wed."

"With all haste, sir," said Renwick.

"I'd say that is recommended," replied the prince, and Georgina blushed.

"Sir!" she said.

"None of your missish ways, my dear. I've heard of you flying off from Rumbridge, and I won't have that kind of thing going on. You'll marry Renwick here and we'll have no more scenes like this."

"Most assuredly not, sir," said Georgina.

"Good," said the prince. "And Renwick."

"Sir?"

"Don't think you'll be able to run back to the north and never appear in London. I'll not be robbed of this lady's company, and command you to come to town."

"I shall obey, sir," said Renwick, smiling.

"Good. Now I shall return to the ball, and you must do so, too. I'll inform your father of your plans." He turned to go, but then paused. "And don't dillydally out here in the garden. You'll be married soon enough."

"Your Royal Highness!" cried Georgina, bursting into laughter. The prince smiled and then retreated.

"Oh, Sam!" cried Georgina, throwing her arms around Renwick again. "He's forgiven us."

"Aye, but I'll not forgive you if you don't cease calling me Sam!" They both laughed, and his lordship locked his lady in a firm embrace and planted a kiss upon her smiling lips.

On Sale in November

"A rich, stirring novel of the westward thrust of America, and of a dynamic woman who went West to tame the wilderness within her."
The Literary Guild

PASTORA
JOANNA BARNES

The passions of two generations, and the rich, colorful history of 19th-century California, are woven into this 768-page epic of adventure and romance! It follows one strong and courageous woman through tragedy and triumph, public scandal and private struggle, as she strives to seize a golden destiny for herself and those she loves!

"Blockbuster historical romance!"
Los Angeles Times

"Readers who like romantic sagas with historical backgrounds will enjoy this."
Library Journal

AVON Paperback   56184 • $3.50

Available wherever paperbacks are sold, or directly from the publisher. Include 50¢ per copy for postage and handling: allow 6-8 weeks for delivery. Avon Books, Mail Order Dept., 224 West 57th St., N.Y., N.Y. 10019.

Pastora 9-81

From

SUSAN ISAACS

**bestselling author of
COMPROMISING POSITIONS
comes a love story
"with three happy endings"**
Washington Post Book World

Close Relations

"Delightful." *Cosmopolitan*

"An exhilarating high."
Los Angeles Times

"Hilarious one minute ... intensely erotic the next ..."
Denver Post

"The love story is tender and satisfying, the plot pulsing with adrenalin."
Publishers Weekly

Susan Isaacs is "a witty, wry observer of the contemporary scene."
The New York Times Book Review

"For a delectable read I recommend entering into close relations with CLOSE RELATIONS."
John Barkham Reviews

AVON Paperback   55681 • $2.95

Available wherever paperbacks are sold, or directly from the publisher. Include 50¢ per copy for postage and handling: allow 6-8 weeks for delivery. Avon Books, Mail Order Dept., 224 West 57th St., N.Y., N.Y. 10019.

Close Relations 9-81